D0888671

Dean Wood is a HGV driver by trade, and can often be found chugging around the Derbyshire countryside. He lives with his wife Julie, step daughter Chloe and Charlie their collie dog. His sister Sharon Wood does the wonderful illustrations that go with his story.

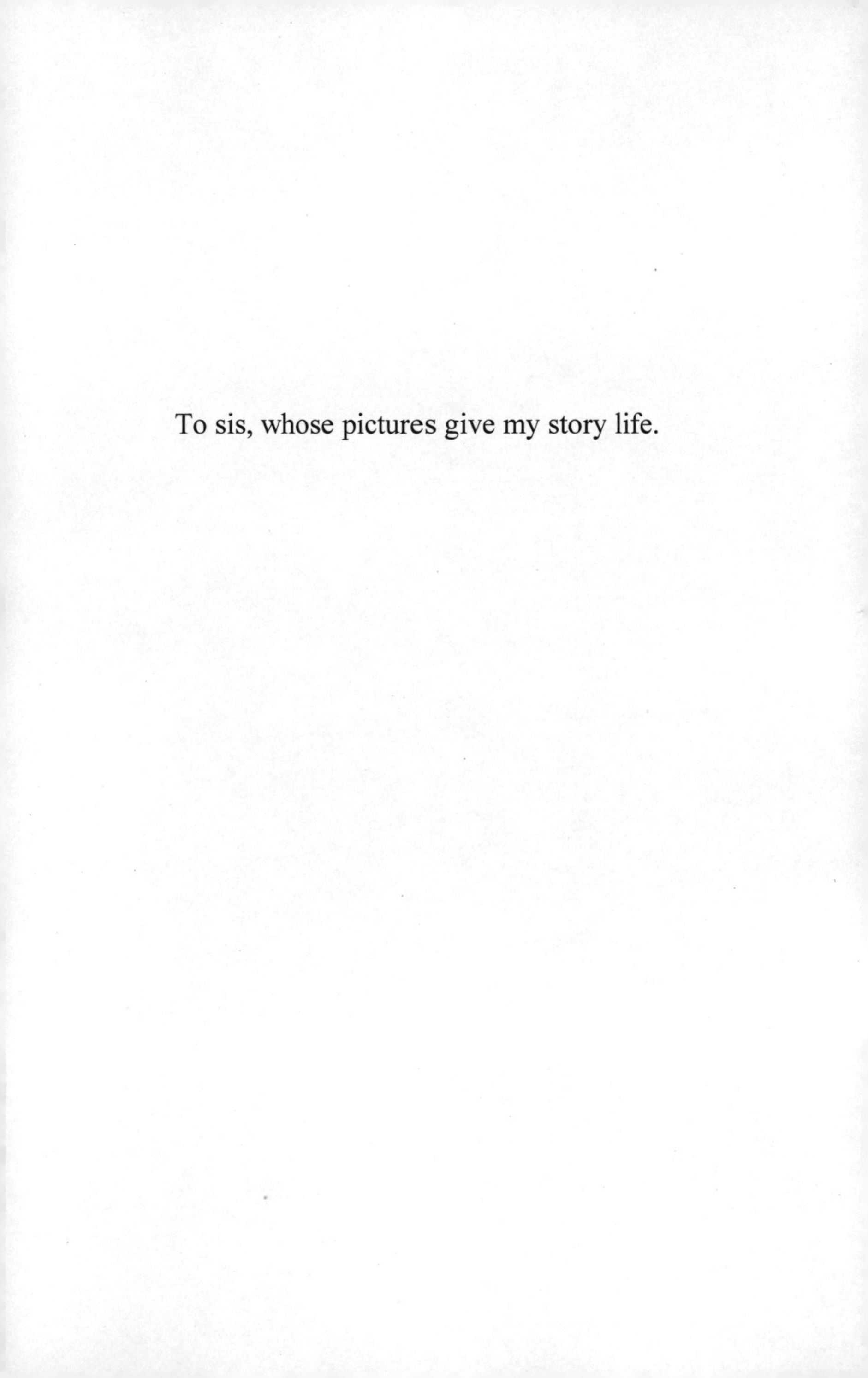

To sis, whose pictures give my story life.

Dean Wood

MICHAEL MOON AND THE CAULDRON OF WISHES

Copyright © Dean Wood

The right of Dean Wood to be identified as author of this work has been asserted by him in accordance with section 77 and 78 of the Copyright, Designs and Patents Act 1988.

All rights reserved. No part of this publication may be reproduced, stored in a retrieval system, or transmitted in any form or by any means, electronic, mechanical, photocopying, recording, or otherwise, without the prior permission of the publishers.

Any person who commits any unauthorized act in relation to this publication may be liable to criminal prosecution and civil claims for damages.

A CIP catalogue record for this title is available from the British Library.

ISBN 978 184963 516 5

www.austinmacauley.com

First Published (2014)
Austin Macauley Publishers Ltd.
25 Canada Square
Canary Wharf
London
E14 5LB

Printed and bound in Great Britain

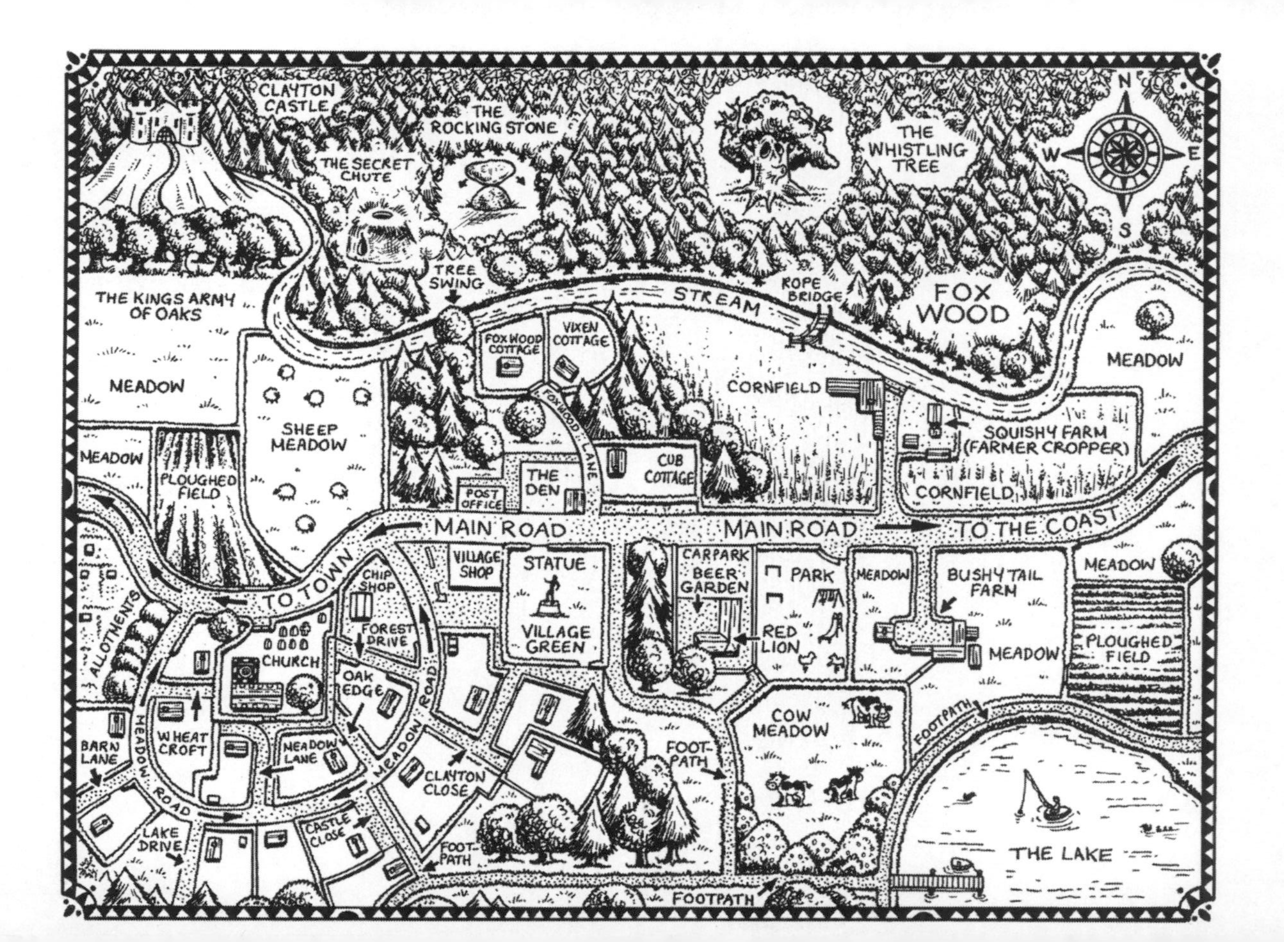

N
W
E
S
CLAYTON CASTLE
THE ROCKING STONE
THE SECRET CHUTE
THE WHISTLING TREE
TREE SWING
STREAM
ROPE BRIDGE
FOX WOOD
THE KINGS ARMY OF OAKS
MEADOW
FOXWOOD COTTAGE
VIXEN COTTAGE
CORNFIELD
MEADOW
SHEEP MEADOW
FOXWOOD LANE
SQUISHY FARM (FARMER CROPPER)
MEADOW
PLOUGHED FIELD
POST OFFICE
THE DEN
CUB COTTAGE
CORNFIELD
MAIN ROAD
MAIN ROAD
TO THE COAST
VILLAGE SHOP
STATUE
CARPARK
BEER GARDEN
PARK
MEADOW
BUSHY TAIL FARM
MEADOW
CHIP SHOP
TO TOWN
VILLAGE GREEN
RED LION
MEADOW
PLOUGHED FIELD
FOREST DRIVE
CHURCH
ALLOTMENTS
OAK EDGE
MEADOW ROAD
COW MEADOW
FOOTPATH
WHEAT CROFT
MEADOW LANE
BARN LANE
CLAYTON CLOSE
FOOT-PATH
MEADOW ROAD
LAKE DRIVE
CASTLE CLOSE
FOOT-PATH
THE LAKE
FOOTPATH

Chapter One

Uncle Ed's Cottage

Michael sat miserably looking down at his new shoes. Great big ugly clomping things they were, but no matter how much he protested to his mother about wearing them, the answer she gave him was always the same.

"Look, stop moaning about them Mickey, I know you like your old trainers better but where we're going they just won't be good enough, you'll need good sturdy shoes like these."

'They're not sturdy, they're clompy,' thought Michael sulkily. He looked across to his baby sister Kizzy who was bolted snugly in her child seat next to him. Her real name was Katherine but everyone had taken to calling her Kizzy. She just sat there, eyes closed as she sucked and chewed merrily on her dummy. She didn't seem upset at all that they were moving to the country. Unlike Michael, he was very upset about having to move home, away from his friends and his school and the city, where there were loads of shops and things to do. Now they were having to move just because Dad had got a stupid new job. Michael sighed, he was going to be stuck in a cottage in the middle of nowhere, with no friends and nothing to do and, worse still, the countryside smells funny too.

Michael felt very bitter and angry, particularly toward his Uncle Ed it was all his stupid fault. It was him that had given Dad the job as manager at his factory that made tractors. Michael couldn't understand why Uncle Ed had given Dad his job, because he had always lived for his tractor factory. It was all he ever talked about, even to the children. So when all of a sudden Michael's dad received a phone call from him saying that he had won the lottery, met a nice young girlfriend and was moving to Monte Carlo, wherever that was, they were all shocked. They were even more surprised when he told them that they could have his country cottage and that Dad would be taking over his precious factory.

Michael sighed deeply, he'd tried to talk Dad out of moving to Uncle Ed's house, but all he said was, "Look Michael, I know you don't want to move, but this is the chance of a life time for us, it's not every day you get to own a factory and a lovely country cottage for nothing."

So that was that, he was just going to have to get used to it.

"Dad, are we nearly there yet?"

"Nearly," replied Dad.

"We'll be there in about twenty minutes Mickey," said Mum.

Just then, upon hearing her favourite name, Kizzy woke up, giggled and roared at the top of her voice, "MEEKY MOOOO!"

Mum and Dad burst out with laughter. Michael on the other hand wasn't amused.

"How many times have I got to tell you, you stupid little girl, my name is Mickey Moon!"

Kizzy just stared at him for a few moments, her big brown eyes twinkling. Then she removed her dummy from her mouth, pointed it straight at Michael and boomed, "MEEKY MOOOO!"

By now Mum was laughing so much she had tears rolling down her face.

“Right that’s it, I’m not talking to any of you anymore!” said Michael angrily, and with that, he folded his arms, turned to look out of the window and sulked for the rest of the journey.

The weather was lovely and sunny as they approached the tiny village of Clayton on the Meadows. Dad drove down the main street that consisted of a village store, a post office, a village green with a statue in the middle and a pub. Just after the post office, dad turned left on to Foxwood Lane. It was a bumpy little track at the bottom of which lay their new home, Foxwood Cottage.

Dad pulled the car on to the gravel drive and parked outside the garage door.

“What do you think of it then?” said Dad as they all climbed out of the car.

Michael looked at the stone cottage. It was the first time he had been to Uncle Ed’s house. It was much bigger than he had expected, much bigger than their squashed up little house in the city. This one had a front garden with a small lawn and a hedge that went all around it. The hedge was covered in lots of different coloured flowers. The garage was big too, big enough for two cars thought Michael.

“It’s quite nice Dad, I like the garden.”

“Yes, well just wait till you see the one around the back,” said Mum.

She led them through a little gate which took them on to a path that went down the side of the cottage and on to the back garden.

“Wow, it’s massive!” said Michael.

The back garden was the biggest he’d ever seen; its lawn was nearly as big as a football pitch. A little stepping stone path led from the back door of the cottage right down the centre of the lawn and stopped half way, where it met a wishing well.

“Is that a real one Dad, with water at the bottom?”

“Yes it is, and it’s very deep, so I don’t want you to go too near to it. If you fall down we may not be able to get you back up, and besides, people around here say there is a troll that lives at the bottom of it," said Dad trying to hide the smirk on his face.

"Yeah, whatever Dad," said Michael.

He didn't believe him for one minute, but all the same he thought he'd better not go too near to it just in case.

The lawn continued to spread out beyond the well until it reached a little fence with an archway that led into an area full of apple trees.

"Wow! Are they real apple trees?"

"Yes, that's our orchard," said Mum.

"Can I climb up and get some please?"

"Yes, but be careful, I don't want you hurting yourself, and don't eat them either, they're for cooking. You'll get an upset tummy if you try to eat them."

At this, Kizzy started giggling again. "Mek Meeky trump trump."

Michael was too interested in what he could get up to in the orchard to be annoyed with Kizzy. He sprinted down the lawn leaving Mum, Dad and Kizzy to go inside and explore their new home. He ran pass the well and through the little gate into the orchard. There were loads of apples on the floor, and some were really big.

'Bigger than cricket balls,' thought Michael. He searched for a moment or two to find a tree with a branch low enough for him to climb on to. Eventually he spotted one near the back of the orchard and clambered up it. He didn't stop climbing until he reached the top where he popped his head out of the branches and looked around. What he saw nearly made him drop out of the tree.

"This is amazing," Michael said to himself; he could see for miles around.

At the back of the orchard there was another small fence with a gate. Just beyond that there was a wide stream, and best of all, it had a proper rope bridge crossing it. Over to his left where the stream was a little narrower, there was a large tree with a rope swing hanging from it. Michael's heart began to race when he thought of all the fun he was going to have exploring his new home. He looked over to his right and could see into next door's garden. Its back lawn looked equally as big as their own and, better still, it had a couple of goalposts set up on it. There was a football left on the lawn. Michael guessed that a little boy must live there; he hoped he could meet him soon and perhaps they could become friends too.

Beyond their neighbour's garden was a large field full of golden barley corn which swayed and shimmered gently in the breeze. 'That would be a great place to play hide and seek,' Michael thought to himself. There were no neighbours to Michael's left, just several gentle rolling meadows, at the far end of which lay a large grassy hill. On top of the hill stood what looked like an ancient castle with turrets and battlements just like the ones he'd seen in the history books at school.

Michael scrambled down the tree as fast as he could, he couldn't wait to tell his parents about the swing, the rope bridge and best of all the medieval castle.

As soon as his feet touched the ground he was sprinting through the orchard. Maybe if there was time his dad could take him to see the castle today. Suddenly Michael's foot struck something in the long grass, it went with a loud bong!! that sent him tumbling head over heels.

"Ouch!" said Michael as he landed amongst the fallen apples with a thump. He sat up and massaged his throbbing big toe as he looked all around him to see what he had tripped on. There in the long grass, just a couple of feet in front of him, lay a large dirty old copper pot, the type you might use for cooking with.

"Grr, stupid thing, where did that come from?"

He couldn't remember seeing it when he ran through the orchard the first time, but then again he'd probably been too interested in finding a tree to climb to notice anything else.

Michael picked himself back up and ran back to the house, this time being a little more careful where he put his feet.

Michael burst through the back door into the kitchen and excitedly told his parents everything he had seen.

His Dad smiled to himself and said, "So you might get to like it here after all then?"

"Yeah, I think it looks really cool around here and I think there may be a little boy living next door too."

"There is, his name's Tony and he's nine years old, the same as you. In fact you will probably be in the same class at school," replied Dad.

"Can we go and visit the castle please Dad?"

"No I'm afraid not. We've got loads of unpacking to do, you included Mickey."

Kizzy opened her mouth ready to roar out her favourite name, but Mum just took the opportunity to shovel in the fork full of baby food that she'd been trying to persuade her to take for the last ten minutes.

"Please Dad," begged Mickey.

"I said no, get off upstairs to your new room and unpack your things, we've taken your case up for you already."

Michael just stood there looking a little disappointed. His Dad noticed and said, "I'll tell you what, when you have done your unpacking and your room is tidy I'll go and get us some fish and chips for supper, deal?"

"Ok Dad, deal."

Michael would have liked to have gone to the castle today, but it was only Friday and he'd have the rest of the weekend to explore. Besides, the thought of fish and chips was making him hungry. So he did as he was told, went upstairs and unpacked his things, all the while dreaming of all the fun and mischief he could get up to tomorrow.

Chapter Two

A New Best Friend

"Mickey… Mickey, are you getting up? It's nine o'clock, I've got breakfast ready for you and your favourite cartoons are on TV."

"Wha, um, er, yeah Mum, I'm coming," said Michael groggily.

He threw the bed sheets off of himself and swung his legs to the left to get out of bed, but as soon as he had done so, his knees made contact with something very hard.

"Ouch! What's going on?" squeaked Michael suddenly much more awake.

Something was wrong; the wall was on the wrong side of the bed. Then suddenly he remembered he was in his new bedroom. He looked over to his right where the sun was pouring in like laser beams through the slits in the blinds. He watched as thousands of tiny dust motes danced and swirled like golden fireflies in the sun's peaceful rays. Michael could hear birds singing too. Hundreds of shrill warbling voices all singing their own song. It sounded so peaceful; he'd never heard birds singing like this before. Living in the city, it was difficult to hear anything above the traffic noise and the constant din of human activity.

Michael wandered over to the window and rolled up the blinds, he had to shield his eyes from the piercing light that suddenly flooded his dim room. Once his eyes had adjusted he looked out of the window at the view. It was lovely, but he couldn't see as much from here as he had from the higher vantage point at the top of the apple tree. He could still see the well, the orchard and the castle on top of the hill, he hadn't dreamt it; it was all real. Just then, he saw a football shoot high in the air over the next door's garden. He couldn't see over the edge from here, but he didn't need to. All that mattered was that the little boy next door was out and he was playing football.

Michael got dressed quickly and thundered down the cottage's steep staircase to the smell of bacon and sausages. He bounded into the kitchen and plonked himself down behind a huge stack of bacon sandwiches.

"Morning Mickey," said Mum, who was stood by the stove holding a frying pan full of fried eggs.

"Morny wum," spluttered Michael through a mouthful of orange juice and soggy sandwiches.

"How many times have I told you not to talk with your mouth full?"

"Sorry. Can I go and call for the boy next door, Mum?"

"Yes, but only when you have finished your breakfast and combed your hair, it looks like a bird's nest."

Dad heaved a great sigh from the corner of the room; he was stood between Kizzy and the portable TV and was trying desperately to get her to eat a spoonful of mushy Weetabix, but was having no joy as she was more interested in cartoons than breakfast.

Michael gobbled his breakfast as quickly as he could, then ran out of the room, pretending not to hear the words "Michael you haven't combed you hair!" as he sprinted down the hall and out through the front door into the early morning sunshine.

Michael made his way over to the house next door. The plaque on their gate read 'Vixen Cottage'. He toddled up the short cobbled stone path and knocked on the front door. After a short while he knocked again and pressed the doorbell.

Bing Bong! Bing Bong! Went the door chime very loudly, so loud it made Michael jump and he began to wonder if the person who answered the door would be angry with him. He need not have feared though, for when the door finally opened, he was greeted by an old man with the friendliest face he had ever seen.

"Hello there, young sir, what can I do for you?" said the old man, staring at Michael.

He seemed to be examining his face very closely as if checking something out.

"Hello, my name is Michael, and I've come to live next door. I was wondering if Tony would like to play football with me, sir?"

"Yes, of course, come through to the back garden and we'll go and ask shall we?"

Michael followed the old man through the house which was very similar in size and the way that the rooms were laid out to their own. But the house's contents and furnishings were very different. Everything looked very old and mysterious. The front room had a large roaring log fire and the floor was made up of ancient-looking flag stones. On the walls, there were many portrait paintings. The people in them wore clothes that ranged from the present time back to the outfits of long ago. Just like the ones he'd seen in his Medieval History lessons. The shelves were full of old leather-bound books and the table was piled high with maps and drawings of strange old contraptions.

The old man led him through the kitchen and into the back garden.

"Toni!... Toni, I've got a young gentleman here that would like to play football with you."

"Ok, coming," replied a rather squeaky voice.

"I'll leave you to it then, have fun both of you," said the old man. Then he turned and shuffled slowly back inside.

Just then, a young girl appeared from around the back of the greenhouse, and came running towards him with a football tucked under her arm.

"Hello," said Michael. "I've come to play football with Tony; you haven't seen him anywhere have you?"

"I'm Toni, nice to meet you," said the little girl holding out a rather grubby looking hand for him to shake.

Michael just stood there, his mouth gaping open with surprise.

"B… B… B… But you're a girl, girls don't play football!"

"Yes they do, well this one does anyway, and I'm as good as any boy!"

"But, I thought you were a boy."

"Yuk! No way, I can't think of anything more gross."

Michael sulkily looked down at his feet. This wasn't fair he thought. He wanted to play football and racing cars, he wanted to play pirates on the river and make rafts and have sword fights. Girls didn't like those sorts of games, they liked dolls and ponies and make-up.

Toni dropped the ball at her feet and looked at Michael with a beaming smile on her face.

"Come on then, let's see if you can get the ball off me!"

"No problem, I'm a really good footballer, so good Dad says that I'll play for England one day," said Michael pointing proudly at the three lions on his new England shirt.

"Ok, prove it Michael Moon," said Toni glancing at the name on the back of his shirt.

"Right, you asked for it!" And, with that, Michael charged at her. But she simply flicked the ball away and side-stepped him.

"Grrr! I'll show you!" said Michael trying again and once more having no luck. In fact, after half an hour of playing he still hadn't managed to get the ball.

"Thought you said you were good," giggled Toni.

"I am. I'm just letting you off because you're a girl and we're playing on your garden that's all."

"Oh really? I believe you, NOT!" said Toni and then started laughing at the sight of Michael standing there sweating, red faced and very angry.

"Well I'm going home now. I don't want to play anymore, besides, my dad said he's going to take me to the castle today, and that's lots more fun than stupid football!"

With that Michael turned to leave.

"No wait, please don't go," said Toni suddenly sounding panicky. "We can play something else, anything you want. I didn't mean to laugh; I think you're a really good footballer. Please stop a bit longer. I haven't got anyone to play with around here."

When Michael saw the miserable expression on Toni's' face, his anger with her immediately disappeared. She looked like she was close to tears.

"Ok, I'll stay. What shall we play?"

"We could play hide and seek in Farmer Cropper's corn field if you like, but whatever you do, don't let him see you. He once caught me in there and lectured me for ages; then he grabbed hold of my ear and dragged me all the way home. It didn't half hurt, and I'm sure that one of my ears has ended up bigger than the other."

Michael burst into a fit of giggles.

"No it hasn't," he said.

"Thank you," replied Toni, looking pleased.

"They're both really big," he said jokingly, and then started laughing again. Toni just blew a raspberry at him.

"Well, I don't think we should play hide and seek then. I don't want to get into trouble on my first day. What about having a go on that tree swing, that looks fun."

"Yes ok, let's go then."

With that, Toni turned to make her way to the gate at the bottom of the garden.

"Hold on, I'll have to let Mum and Dad know where I'm going. Aren't you going to let your granddad know what we're up to before we go?"

"No, he's ok as long as I don't go any further than the tree swing, and besides, he's not my granddad, he's my dad."

"Oh!" said Michael surprised. "But he looks really old."

"Yes, so what? That doesn't stop him being my dad, he adopted me actually, which I think is a very nice thing to do."

"Yes it was, he seems very nice," said Michael backtracking quickly, as he could see that he'd offended her.

"Yes, well, anyway, are we going to play on that swing or what?"

"Ok, I'll race you! Last one to the gate is pants at football," said Michael, and took off down the lawn as fast as he could, with Toni chasing after him.

The two children played happily on the tree swing for hours and when they were tired of that, they climbed the trees in the orchard. Then, finally, they went up stream to the rope bridge where they had races with the sticks that they threw in the water.

Michael didn't even bother going to the castle when his dad offered to take him. He was having way too much fun with his new friend.

At six o' clock, Toni's' dad shouted her in for her tea.

"Are you coming out to play again tomorrow?"

"Yeah, you bet, today has been brill. You know you're really good fun, for a girl!"

"Thanks, you're not so bad yourself, for a boy!"

Then Toni blew another raspberry at him and ran off home.

Michael smiled to himself, he'd had the most fun he could ever remember having, and who would have thought that his new best friend would have been a girl.

Chapter Three

The Magic Cauldron

Michael was woken by his mum knocking on his bedroom door at nine o'clock on Sunday morning.

"Mickey, Toni's here to see you; are you getting up or shall I tell her to come back again later?"

"No, I'm getting up," said Michael leaping out of bed and running down stairs in his pyjamas.

"Hello Toni, I won't be long, I've just got to get changed and then I'll be with you."

"You're not going anywhere until you've had some breakfast," said Dad from behind his newspaper.

"Would you like some breakfast Toni, there's plenty of toast and honey?"

"No thank you Mr Moon. I've already had some breakfast," Toni replied.

Michael scoffed his two slices of toast and a glass of orange juice as fast as he could. Then he quickly got changed and came back down stairs and rejoined everyone back in the kitchen.

"Are we ready to go then, MEEKY MOO?" said Toni with a wicked smirk on her face.

Michael could tell by the way that his paper was shaking, that Dad must have been laughing the other side of it. Mum just stuck her head deep into one of the cupboards and pretended to be looking for something.

"You again!" said Michael, spinning around and fixing Kizzy with an angry stare.

"Why did I have to have a baby sister, why couldn't we have had a puppy or something nice like that?"

"Because puppies are noisy, smelly and make lots of mess," replied Mum.

"Well she's noisy, smelly and makes lots of mess."

"Now, now, Michael, there's no need to be like that. You know Kizzy thinks the world of you. Look! She wants you to give her a hug."

Michael looked down to where Kizzy was sat on the floor surrounded by cuddly toys and dolls. She was looking up at him with a big broad smile on her face and was holding her arms out toward him beckoning him for a hug. Michael took pity on her and bent down to pick her up. He lifted her so that they were face to face, smiled and tickled her chin. Kizzy giggled with delight.

"You're not so bad really I suppose."

Just then, without warning, Kizzy swung the baby rattle she'd been brandishing in her hand, and began to pound Michael's earhole with it.

"AAAARRRGH!" screamed Michael as he ran across the kitchen and deposited Kizzy into his mother's arms.

"Here, you have the horrible little thing, I'm going out!"

He stamped off outside with Toni following, barely able to walk with laughter.

"I don't see what's so funny, you wouldn't like it if I did it to you," Michael fumed.

"Just try it, and I'll give you a big red tab on the other side of your head as well," giggled Toni.

Michael opened his mouth to say something and then thought better of it. He could see already that Toni was very tough, and if he had thought that being beaten at football by a girl was bad enough, then the idea of finishing second to one in a tussle was more than he could bear.

"Well, what shall we do then Toni?"

"I've been wanting to go fishing for ages. We could do that if you like."

"Er, yeah, that would be great, but I haven't got a fishing rod, have you?"

"Yes, sort of, it's a fishing net on a stick. It's in the garage at home."

"I've never been fishing before," said Michael.

"I have, but I've only fished in the stream around the back of our gardens, and there can't be many fish in there as I've never managed to catch one. I thought we could have a walk up to the lake. I know there's fish in there because I've seen men pulling fish out of the water loads of times. We just need something to put in all the fish we catch."

"I've got just the thing; I found an old copper cooking pot in the orchard. If we cleaned it up it would be perfect."

"Great, that's it then, let's get ready and go."

"Erm, is the lake far away, I'm not sure Mum and Dad will let me go if it is?"

"No it's not far; it's at the bottom of the meadow behind the pub. It's less than ten minutes away. Hey, we could even call at the shop and get some pop and crisps. We could make it a picnic if you'd like?"

Michael agreed, he felt really excited; he'd only ever been on picnics in the garden with Mum, Dad and Kizzy. So, once the two children had told their parents where they were going and they had gathered up everything they needed, they set off for the lake. They walked up Foxwood Lane toward the main road where the grocer's shop, post office and pub were all to be found.

"I'll race you, last one to the shop buys the picnic," said Toni as she began to make a dash across the road.

"Whoa!" screamed Michael. He grabbed hold of the waistband of Toni's tracksuit bottoms and pulled her back as hard as he could, just in time to be missed by the little red car that went speeding by, hooting its horn loudly as it went.

"Are you flipping bonkers or something? Didn't anyone ever tell you to look both ways before crossing?"

Toni just stood there, wide-eyed and trembling as she realised just how close she had come to being run over. It took a moment or two before either of them spoke.

Eventually, Toni said, "Thank you," and smiled shyly at him. She then walked over and gave him a big hug.

"Hey, geroff!" said Michael feeling uncomfortable. "Let's go and get that picnic, I'm starving."

Michael and Toni crossed the road and entered the village store. It was gloomy inside and it took a minute or two for Michael's eyes to adjust to the dimly lit little room.

"Wow! It's like Aladdin's' Cave in here," said Michael as he looked around.

The shop was packed floor to ceiling with every different kind of goods you could ever possibly want, from bread and milk to magazines, from biscuits to bike pumps; petrol cans, carpet slippers or shiny garden tools. At the far end of the shop, barely visible for all the clutter, was the counter, on which stood a very large antique till. As the children approached the counter, a small white bubble-permed head popped out from behind the till. The old lady beamed at them through very thick horn-rimmed spectacles.

"Hello Toni, what can I do for you and your handsome new friend today?"

"Hello, this is my new friend Mickey; he lives next door to me now. He's very nice but he's not very good at football, so we decided to go fishing at the lake today and we've come to get some food for a picnic."

"Is that so? Well you've certainly picked a lovely day for it. I hope you catch lots of fish."

"Me too," said Michael. "I've never been fishing before, so I hope we can catch lots of fish and then we'll put them all in here," he said, holding up the copper pot for the old lady to see.

Her smile disappeared instantly and her eyes bulged in surprise and shock. She looked for all the world like she'd seen a ghost.

"W…w…where on earth did you get that thing from?" she stuttered.

"Erm, I found it in our orchard, is it yours?" said Michael, suddenly feeling a lot less proud of his discovered treasure.

"It most certainly is not, and if you take my advice, you'll put it right back where you found it or better still throw it in the lake," said the old woman as she came from around the counter and began to shoo the children out of her shop.

"Go on get out of here and don't ever bring that thing in here again. My word, and you being Harry Millward's daughter as well. You should know better. Go on shoo, the pair of you!"

"But what about our picnic stuff? We haven't paid for it yet," squeaked Toni.

"Never mind that it's on the house. Just get out!"

The two children scuttled out of the shop's front doors as fast as they could.

"Wow, she's barmy," said Michael.

"She's never been like that before, she's usually very nice. She must really dislike that pot."

"It's not that bad, a bit dirty perhaps but I thought it was cool."

"Well something about it must have really freaked her out to let us have the picnic food without paying for it. She's usually as quick as Scrooge when it comes to taking your money," said Toni shrugging her shoulders and turning away from the shop.

Toni led Michael on to the footpath which took them around the back of the Red Lion pub and into the meadows beyond. There were cows in the field and Michael watched them with interest as they slowly chomped their way through the grass. He was just thinking to himself what lovely peaceful creatures they looked, when one of them sneaked up behind him and gave a very loud MOOOO, in his ear. This made him jump and sent him scuttling behind Toni for protection.

At the bottom of the meadow they reached the little stile which they clambered over and took to the gravel path which led them down to the pier at the water's edge. As they passed by the hedgerows, Michael noticed a large colourful insect with huge buzzing wings.

"What's that Toni?"

"A dragonfly silly, haven't you seen one before?"

Finally they reached the little wooded pier, which stretched out into the lake before them. Tethered to the left-hand side of the pier was a wooden boat that knocked gently against its moorings as it bobbed up and down in the lapping water.

"This place is Heaven," said Michael.

"I know, it's my special place, no one ever seems to come here but me. You won't go telling everyone at school about it will you because it's a secret?"

"No, I won't. Not if you don't want me to, I'm a man of my word," said Michael proudly puffing out his chest. Toni looked him in the eye and decided that she trusted him.

"Ok then, I believe you, let's spit and shake hands on it."

"Erm, yes ok," said Michael offering out his hand. Much to his horror, Toni gobbed out a large mouthful of spit into her palm and then clamped her hand firmly to his.

"Ew, you really are the strangest girl I've ever met."

Toni just giggled as she sat herself down and dangled her legs over the end of the pier. Michael sat down beside her and watched as she dipped the fishing net into the clear water. He couldn't help but notice how pretty Toni was. Her chestnut brown hair which was tied into short braids on either side of her head, fluttered gently in the morning breeze. She had vivid green eyes which were always soft and smiling, and her small freckly nose crinkled whenever she laughed. Her clothes though, were far from girlish and were pretty similar to his own. In fact he really liked the football shirt she was wearing and wondered which team it belonged to.

"Toni, will I be in your class at school?"

"I don't know; who's your teacher?"

"I think it said Mr Scrimshaw on the letter we had from school."

"You're in the other class then, I'm in Mrs Doogle's class."

"Oh," said Michael disappointedly. "I hope the other kids are nice to me, there aren't any bigger boys in my class are there?"

"Er, well, there is one, his name is Charlie Bowler, but you'll be ok if you stay out of his way."

"Charlie Bowler," squeaked Michael, a sense of dread beginning to wash over him.

"Yeah, Chunky Charlie, but don't worry he's too big to be able to run fast, and even if he does catch you, he'll just sit on your chest until you give him your dinner money."

"He sounds horrible, I don't think I want to go to school anymore," said Michael, his bottom lip trembling.

"You'll be alright," said Toni seeing that Michael was getting very upset. "I'll stick up for you, I promise."

Michael said nothing; he just sat there worrying about Chunky Charlie. Toni passed him the fishing net.

"Here, you have a go, I don't think I'm very good at this," she said, hoping that this might cheer him up a little.

A short time later, after they still hadn't managed to catch any fish, Michael suggested that they start their picnic. He jammed the pole of the fishing net between two of the pier's deck boards, grabbed the carrier bag full of snacks, emptied it out and shared the contents out equally between them. He was just about to sink his teeth into his bar of chocolate when something in the water caught his eye.

"Hey, I think I just saw a fish," he said, jumping to his feet.

"Quick, fill your pot full of water just in case we catch one," spluttered Toni through a mouthful of crisps.

Michael grabbed the pot, filled it from the lake and ran over to where Toni was stood, excitedly swishing the fishing net through the water. Nothing happened for a few minutes and then suddenly the object floated back into view a couple of inches away from Toni's fishing net.

"There it is, there, there, quick look," shouted Michael jumping up and down. Toni squinted and peered more closely at the object Michael was pointing at.

"That's not a fish you idiot, it's an old carrier bag."

"Well I didn't know, I've never been fishing before, it looked like a fish from here."

"In that case, I think you should get yourself some specs."

"Shut up," grumbled Michael.

"Ooh look, there's a baby fish over there," said Toni pointing to an empty crisp packet that had come floating into view from under the pier.

"Shut up, you're not funny," and, with that, Michael turned his back on her and sat himself down with a thump as if to put a full stop on the end of their argument. He sat crossed legged in front of his pot and peered miserably into it. He saw his glum reflection staring straight back at him. He stuck his hand inside the pot and stirred the water so as to break up the image.

"I'm sorry, I didn't mean to make fun, you're still speaking to me aren't you?" said Toni from somewhere behind him.

"Humpfff, suppose so," he said giving her a quick backward glance and then returning to sitting face forwards, with his back straight and arms folded across his chest. He glanced downward at the pot and then gasped in amazement when he saw that water had not settled but had continued to swirl and was now spinning with so much speed that it had turned into a whirlpool like the ones he'd seen go down the bathtub plughole.

"Whoa, Toni, quick come over here and look at this."

"What is it this time, a killer whale doing back flips?"

"I'm not kidding, just get here now," said Michael as he watched the swirling water that had now turned luminous green. Toni ran over to see what all the fuss was about and then dropped to her knees with shock when she saw the bizarre contents of the pot.

"W…what have you done to make it do that?"

"Nothing, I just put my hand in the water and then it started doing this."

They watched as the water slowly stopped spinning and then began to bubble furiously. Eventually the liquid settled and the bright green surface became as smooth as glass, and then the most amazing thing happened. Dozens of tiny orange letters appeared on the surface. At first they moved about randomly, bumping and bouncing off one another but eventually they came to rest and formed a sentence which read:

"To my new owner, Congratulations, you have found the Magic Cauldron."

Michael and Toni stood facing one another, their eyes bulging and their mouths gaping open in surprise. Then suddenly Toni's expression changed and a wry smile spread across her face.

"Hang on, you knew this was going to happen all along didn't you?"

"Eh, what? How could I possibly know that this was going to happen, what are you talking about Toni?"

"Nah, you're not fooling me, this is one of your toys isn't it? I bet it's got batteries or something."

Toni went to pick up the cauldron to check underneath for a battery compartment, but the instant her fingers made contact with it, the cauldron violently spat out a jet of stinking hot luminous green water which hit her smack in the face. She jumped back with a terrified squeal. Michael looked into the pot and saw that the letters had formed into another sentence.

"A warning to all, only he or she who stirred my waters can call themselves my owner. Only he or she may touch me."

"Fine, I don't want to touch it anyway, it seems dangerous to me; no wonder old Elsie from the shop freaked out when she clapped eyes on it. She must have seen it before."

Michael just ignored her. He reached out slowly with a shaking hand and touched the cauldron. The words reformed once more:

"Greetings Meeky Moo."

"Oh for goodness sake, not you as well," said Michael not knowing whether to be afraid or annoyed.

"I am to be your servant for the next four days; I will grant you four wishes, one on each day. Be warned, choose wisely."

Michael just sat there trembling, not knowing what he should do next. Toni, on the other hand, was beginning to get annoyed and more than a little bit jealous.

"It won't work you know, and even if it does I bet you my last gobstopper that it will be trouble."

She walked to the end of the pier and stood miserably looking out over the lake.

"What's wrong?" enquired Michael after a few moments of silence had passed.

"Nothing."

"Yes there is, you seem sad."

"Well it's not fair, nothing exciting ever happens to me at all, all I wanted to do was catch some fish and now that you have found that cauldron you won't want to catch fish or play with me anymore."

Michael felt sorry for Toni; he didn't like to see anyone upset, least of all his friends. So, he decided there and then that his first wish would be something to cheer her up. He couldn't think of anything at first and then suddenly an idea came to him. He peered down into the cauldron and said out loud:

"I wish that my friend Toni could catch loads of fish."

The cauldron instantly started to bubble and hiss and the water turned from bright green to vivid red. When it settled, snowy white letters appeared on the surface. They jostled about until they read:

"Your wish is granted."

Then the liquid turned back into ordinary water. Toni ran up to Michael and gave him a big hug.

"Thank you for using your first wish on me, that was very kind of you."

"No problem, you're welcome. Just let go of me please, you're squeezing the breath out of me."

Toni giggled and let go of him.

"Come on, let's get your fishing net back in the water," said Michael.

He picked up the fishing net, scampered over to the end of the pier and plunged it into the water. He swished the net about excitedly, expecting a really big fish to swim straight into it but nothing happened. Five minutes passed and still there was no sign of any fish. Michael turned to Toni, disappointment written all over his face.

"I'm sorry, it looks like you were right, I don't think it's going to work, maybe it's some kind of clever toy after all."

"Hmmm, let me have a go," said Toni, her face all screwed up with concentration. "I think it might work for me, remember your wish was, 'I wish *my friend Toni* could catch loads of fish.'"

"Oh yeah, that's right, here catch," said Michael throwing the fishing net to Toni.

She caught it and eagerly dipped it into the lake. As soon as the net was in the water, a large fish swam straight into it. She dragged the fishing net out with a squeal of delight and plopped the fish into the pot full of water. Then she had another go and instantly caught another big fat gleaming fish.

"Wow, this is brill, I wish Dad could see me now, he likes fishing I think he'd be really proud of me."

Toni continued to sink her fishing net into the water and every rime that she did, she was rewarded with a catch, each one bigger and more beautiful than the last. Soon the pot was filled to the brim with fish. Toni stood beaming at Michael.

"Ooh, that was such good fun."

"Yeah, it was mega, you looked like a real life fisherman catching all of those fish, but what are we going to do with them now?"

"Well, I suppose we should throw them all back, It's just a pity that Dad didn't get to see them," said Toni sadly.

"Hey, my mobile phone takes pictures, I'll take a photo of you and your fish and then we can show it to him when we get back home."

"Yeah, great, have you got it with you?"

"Yup, it's here, say cheese."

Toni stood and posed while Michael took a few photographs and then Michael joined her and stood with the phone at arm's length and took a picture containing both of them. Then they emptied all of the fish back into the lake and began to make their way back home.

"Toni, I don't think we should tell anybody about the magic cauldron, do you?"

"Erm, well what about our parents, don't you think we should tell them?"

"No, they'll confiscate it, you know what grownups are like, they'll spoil our fun."

"Yes you're probably right, we'll keep it secret; what are you going to wish for next?"

"I don't know yet, but whatever I do wish for, it's sure to be loads of fun."

Chapter Four

Michael's Big Day at School

That night Michael sat watching Sunday evening TV with his parents. Some of his favourite programmes were on but he found he couldn't concentrate on them. His mind kept wandering back to all the fun he'd had with his new friend and in particular the magic cauldron and his three remaining wishes. He couldn't decide what to wish for, there were so many things that he would like. A lifetime's supply of pop and chocolate would be nice, but then again so would a brand new mountain bike or a little puppy. Most of all he wanted to play for the England football team although he thought that perhaps he needed to be a bit bigger first.

As the evening wore on thoughts of his magic cauldron began to fade and fear of his first day at his new school began to creep in. Michael was terrified he was going to get bullied. He'd always been picked on at school due to the fact that he was quite small and thin for his age, but at least at his old school he knew who the bullies were and where he could hide from them. He'd had a few friends there too who would often stick up for him if things got really bad.

"Are you all right Michael? You're very quiet tonight," said his mum who was sat cuddled up to his dad on the sofa.

"No Mum, I'm not alright, I've got a really bad belly ache and I think I'm going to be sick too."

His parents just exchanged knowing glances at one another.

"We'll give you some medicine for your tummy before you go to bed, then you should be as fit as a fiddle for school in the morning," said Mum.

"B…but I'm really ill, there's no way I'm going to be fit for school tomorrow, why don't you believe me?"

"We do believe you, I'm sure you have got the belly ache but I think it's probably a symptom of you getting yourself wound up about school tomorrow," said his dad.

"B…but Dad it really hurts."

"Look Michael, please don't make me cross with you, it's school in the morning and that's that, end of story. In fact it's about time you were going to bed; don't forget to brush your teeth first."

Michael looked at his mum, his bottom lip was trembling and he began to cry. It had the desired effect, as she got up and came over to give him a cuddle.

"Come on Michael, I'll take you up to bed and read you a story."

"Ok Mum," sniffed Michael.

"Here, I'll give you a piggy back."

So he jumped on his mum's back and the two of them trotted off up the stairs. After he'd cleaned his teeth, his mum tucked him up in bed, all warm and cosy, just how he liked it. She was just about to start reading him his favourite book when she spotted the cauldron standing on his desk beneath the window.

"Ooooh, what's that?"

"It's just a pot I found in the orchard," said Michael dismissively.

"Hmmm, that would look really good on my stove; I could get a lot of vegetables in there."

"No Mum it's mine, I found it and I need it because, erm, I'm going to use it as a piggy bank for all my pocket money."

His mum just smiled, agreed, and then read him two chapters of his bedtime story. After she'd finished, she leaned forward and kissed his forehead and said goodnight to him. But Michael was still wide awake.

"Mum, if I'm poorly in the morning please don't make me go to school."

His mum heaved a huge weary sigh.

"Let's see what the morning brings shall we?"

"Ok, thanks Mum," said Michael feeling a little more cheerful now that he thought he was getting his own way.

His mum left him alone with his night light, to drift off to sleep, but very soon it seemed he was beginning to have strange and scary nightmares about a huge boy who sat on his chest and repeatedly slapped his face with a big wet fish until Michael promised to give up his dinner money and his new England shirt. He awoke with a shout, covered in sweat and was trembling. He called out in the darkness to his parents, and very soon he heard footsteps on the landing outside his room. Then the door opened and in walked Dad in his pyjamas. He was yawning and his hair was ruffled.

"Dad, I had a bad dream."

"I know son, I heard you shouting, are you alright?"

"No Dad, I'm really scared of going to school in the morning. There's a bully there, his name is Chunky Charlie and he steals people's dinner money."

"I'm sure that's not true," said his father with a slight smirk on his face.

"It is; Toni told me."

"Well if he does do anything to you, go straight to your teacher and tell them what happened and if that fails you could always tell him your big daddy will come around and sort him out."

His dad sat up straight, puffed out his chest and flexed his muscles like the strongmen on the TV. Michael giggled.

"I wish I was as big as you Dad, then Chunky Charlie would have to look out, I'd knock his block clean off."

"That's my boy," said Dad ruffling Michael's hair. "Now off to sleep again, it's gone midnight."

"Can I have my light on please?"

"Yes of course." His dad got up and made for the door.

"Oh and Dad, can I have a drink of water?"

"You've already got one."

"I want a fresh one."

"MICHAEL, GOODNIGHT!" With that, his dad stomped off shutting the bedroom door behind him. Michael just sighed; he plumped his pillow then turned over on to his side and tried to go to sleep. He was just starting to drift off to sleep when he was awoken by a loud bubbling noise coming from over by the window. He sat up and peered over the top of the teddy bear's head that he was cuddling and saw the cauldron wobbling and bouncing about on top of his desk. He leapt out of bed and ran over to the cauldron to see what it was doing. Michael looked down at the contents of the pot and saw that the fluid was cherry red and that the white letters were once more beginning to form a message which said:

"Your wish is granted!"

Michael felt confused, he hadn't wished for anything and he didn't think he was due another wish until tomorrow. Just then, Michael felt the waistband of his pyjamas begin to tighten and when he looked down to see why this was happening, he noticed the legs of his pyjama bottoms were shrinking and the arms of his top were too. Michael squeaked in panic and he began removing his night attire as fast as he could as they were rapidly becoming painfully tight. He stood there trembling with fear; he was at a loss to know why his PJs had shrunk. He turned to make a run for the door and saw his reflection in the mirror of his wardrobe. Michael suddenly realised what was happening. It wasn't his pyjamas that had shrunk, it was he that had grown bigger, much bigger; in fact he now looked as big as his dad.

"Doh, of course," said Michael slapping himself on the forehead.

He'd said to his dad when he had come to comfort him that he wished he was as big as him. He also remembered his dad telling him to go to sleep as it was gone midnight, which meant that it was now Monday morning, day two, wish two.

"Ooh this feels weird," thought Michael still staring at himself in the mirror. He was now as big as a full-grown man but he still bore the features of a nine year old boy. He giggled when he looked at the size of his feet.

"Whoa, look at these monsters, if Chunky Charlie picks on me he's going to get one of these right up the back of his pants."

His initial fears about his first day at school were receding and instead he was now feeling excited at the thought of all the fun he was going to have in his giant new body. He couldn't wait to see the look on his parents' and Toni's faces when they saw him in the morning. He climbed into bed feeling much happier and even laughed when his feet and ankles popped out of the bottom of the bedsheets and hung over the end of his bed. Michael quickly drifted off to sleep and didn't wake up again until the alarm clock on his bedside drawers announced the start of a new day with its loud beeping. He awoke with a start and shot out his hand to switch off the horrible racket. Instead, his hand struck the clock much sooner than he had expected and sent it tumbling across the bedroom. He'd forgotten that his arms were now much longer than they used to be. Michael climbed out of bed yawning deeply, and sloped over to the wardrobe to retrieve his school uniform. On seeing it, he realised it wasn't going to fit. Mum and Dad weren't going to be pleased. He didn't know what to do next, so he shouted down to his father.

"Dad, I'm not going to be able to go to school today because my uniform doesn't fit."

There came a fair bit of mumbling and moaning from downstairs before his father replied.

"Grrrr, Michael get dressed, you're not getting out of school that easily."

"But Dad, it really doesn't fit."

"Of course it blooming well fits. We only bought it two weeks ago. If you're not dressed and down here in five minutes, there's no pocket money."

Five minutes passed and still there was no sign of Michael, so his dad shouted up to him again.

"Michael, are you dressed? You'd better be, otherwise you're going to be late for school."

"Dad, I'm telling the truth. My uniform doesn't fit me."

"Right, that's it, I'm coming up there and I'm going to dress you myself just like a little baby."

Michael heard the thump, thump of his dad's feet pounding the stairs, the noise getting ominously ever closer. His dad flung open the bedroom door and stepped into the room, ready to have a blazing row with his son, but was stunned into silence, when instead he found himself staring eye to eye with him.

"Morning, Pops," boomed Michael in a deep manly voice.

His dad just stood there with his eyes bulging, and his mouth silently opening and closing like a goldfish. When, eventually, he did manage to recover his voice, the only noise he could make was a very loud and girly "Eeeeek!"

He then turned and fled down the stairs as fast as his legs could carry him.

Michael collapsed on to his bed in a fit of laughter. Today was going to be a really funny day, he could see that already. He got up and lolloped down the stairs after his dad. He was about halfway down when his head suddenly made contact with a particularly low roof beam.

"Ooooh ek, I'll have to remember to duck for that one in future," said Michael rubbing the spot on his head where a large lump was beginning to blossom. From where he stood, Michael could hear his parents arguing from the kitchen.

"You do talk rubbish sometimes Steven. How on earth can he possibly have grown that much over night?"

"Emma, I'm serious, he's flippin' massive; he's as big as me!"

"Oh, ha ha, it's not April Fool's Day, you know."

Just then Michael bounded into the kitchen and positively roared at his mother.

"HELLO MUM!"

Mum stood there wearing the same goldfish expression that previously his dad had worn. Then suddenly she too emitted a loud terrified "Eeeeek!"

Although, perhaps not quite as high-pitched and girly as his dad's had been. The only member of the family that didn't seem too concerned about Michael's accelerated growth spurt was Kizzy. She just sat in her booster chair at the table with her arms outstretched begging him for a cuddle.

"Come here little girl," said Michael suddenly feeling very manly, as he swept his tiny sister up into his big strong arms.

"Whoa, this is getting too weird, I'm going to call the doctor," said Michael's dad.

"Good idea, maybe he'll be able to tell us what has happened to him. Do you think it's something we've fed him that's caused this?" said Mum.

"And you accused me of talking rubbish, how could this possibly be caused by something he ate? Honestly that's the daftest thing you ever said," roared Dad.

"Don't call me daft Steven, or else you'll be wearing your omelette for a hat!"

"Here Mum, you'd better take Kizzy, I think her nappy needs changing," interjected Michael in a booming voice as he held out his little sister at arm's length.

"I'm really hungry this morning, I think I'm going to need extra rations, I'm a growing lad you know," teased Michael.

"Good grief, I'd not thought of that, he's going to eat us out of house and home. I'd better put some more time in at the tractor factory."

"Yes, and I'm going to have to go shopping and buy him an entire new wardrobe of clothes," said Mum, suddenly looking stressed.

"Dad, I've changed my mind about school today, I'd really like to go. Do you think I could borrow some of your clothes?"

Michael's parents looked at each other uncertainly as they considered what to do with their oversized son. Eventually his mum decided that it would be a good idea if he went to school. But first she was going to write a letter for him to take to his teacher explaining why he wasn't wearing a school uniform.

Whilst she did this Michael went upstairs with his dad and chose some clothes from his wardrobe. He was given his father's best going out clothes, which consisted of a white shirt, black trousers, shiny black shoes and a very smart jacket. Michael couldn't believe how grown up he looked. It felt really weird wearing adult clothing, he thought to himself. He thanked his dad and then went next door to call for Toni. His parents had agreed with Toni's dad that they would take it in turns each week to take the children to school to help save money on petrol.

Michael pressed the button for the doorbell and flinched again at the horrifyingly loud, bing bong chime that it made. From the other side of the door he heard rapid footsteps coming down the stairs. Then Toni shouted to her father.

"See you later Dad, have a good day."

She flung open the door and rushed outside only to bump face first into her once pint-sized pal's belly.

"Whoops, watch where you're going little girl," said Michael in his booming voice as he patted her on the head.

For a moment or two he was treated to his third goldfish impression of the day, but then she shook her head so as to clear her thoughts and a big grin slowly spread across her face.

"I'm guessing that wish number two was that you wanted to be big?"

"Got it in one; you're really quite clever aren't you, for a little girl that is."

"Yes I am, and stop calling me little girl or else I'll tell everyone at school that your nickname is Meeky Moo!"

"Ok, ok, deal. Anyway we'd better get a move on. Mum said she was ready to take us to school."

The two of them rushed back to Michael's house just in time to catch his mum coming out of the front door with Kizzy in her arms. She unlocked the car and strapped Kizzy safely into her car seat. Michael sat in the front with Mum whilst Toni buckled herself into the seat behind Michael. Toni was really excited. She'd never travelled in a car before as her dad's eyesight was so poor it prevented him from getting a driving licence. Instead he always accompanied her to school on the bus. As his mum pulled out of the drive, they passed the milkman. He looked directly at them and much to everyone's amazement he didn't seem the slightest bit surprised at the sight of a mother with her six foot, nine year old son. It was the same when the postman caught sight of them too. He just smiled, waved and then carried on delivering the post.

"That's odd, anyone would think they were used to seeing huge man-sized children around here," said Michael's mum frowning.

She pulled the car up outside the village store and told Michael to go and get himself some credit for his mobile phone.

"Wait for me, I'll come with you," said Toni as she unbuckled her seatbelt and jumped out of the car.

As they entered the shop they immediately spotted the white bubble-permed helmet of old Elsie protruding above the till. Her eyes magnified many times by her spectacles never left the children as they approached the counter.

"Well, well, it looks like you've found out what that old cauldron's for. I'm presuming that you didn't follow my advice about throwing it in the lake and that you're still in possession of the wicked thing."

"Erm, yes I do still have it, but you won't tell our parents will you?"

"I bloomin' well should do young man. That cauldron is no toy and it's brought a lot of people around here nothing but trouble for centuries. If you take my advice you will choose your remaining wishes very carefully."

"Do you think my dad will have heard about this cauldron?" said Toni.

"Oh yes, he's heard about it alright. I should have thought that he of all people would have something to say about your little find."

"What do you mean Mrs Arkwright, are you trying to tell me that he's been the owner of the cauldron at some point?" said Toni.

"I'm not saying another word. In fact I've said far too much already. Please purchase what you came in for and then be gone. All this talk of the magic cauldron has made me come over all funny."

Michael bought the credit for his phone with the five pounds his mum had given him, and then the two of them left the shop as quickly as their legs could carry them.

"That old lady really freaks me out. Hey, I wonder what she meant about your dad having a story to tell about the cauldron."

"Hmmm, I don't know but I'm going to ask him about it when I get home tonight."

Toni was very quiet for the rest of the journey to school. Michael tried to make conversation with her on several occasions but she didn't seem to be listening. It was obvious that she was worrying about something. Michael asked her what was wrong but she wouldn't reply to him until his mum had dropped them off outside the school gates.

"Michael, I don't think you should make any more wishes with that cauldron, at least not until we've found out more about it. I'm beginning to suspect that it really is dangerous."

"Oh come on, don't tell me old Elsie has spooked you. I can't see what harm it can do, as long as you don't wish for anything bad then nothing bad will happen."

Toni was just about to open her mouth and protest when she suddenly became aware of the crowd that was rapidly assembling around them. Mothers and children alike were stood open mouthed staring at him.

"Hey knock it off will you, didn't anyone tell you it's rude to stare?" boomed Michael in his baritone voice.

Many of them quickly turned and walked away whispering to one another as they went. Some just continued to stare, and worst of all one little girl just buried her face in her mother's chest and burst into tears. Michael suddenly started to feel uncomfortable and out of place as he stood in a playground full of children half his size.

"Come on let's get you to your classroom before anyone else turns up to have a nosy at you."

Toni took him by the hand and marched him toward the main building, looking for all the world as if she were his daughter.

"Just wait here for a minute, please; I need to go to the toilet before the lessons start."

"Ok, but don't be long. I don't want to be on my own."

Toni left Michael standing by the main doors to the school building and rounded the corner in the direction of the girls' toilets. Unfortunately, she was in so much of a rush that she failed to notice the big pink lump of flesh that was Chunky Charlie. She walked straight into him, knocking his can of pop flying. One or two of his cronies that were hanging around began to laugh, but were silenced immediately when Charlie shot them a thunderous look.

"Watch where you're going tom boy; that will be your dinner money that you owe me to pay for my pop."

"No way Charlie, that's not fair, my dinner money comes to a lot more than the price of a can of pop."

"You should have thought of that before you came barging into me shouldn't you? Now cough up or I'll take it by force anyway, and just for good measure I'll snip your pigtails off too!"

Toni suddenly made a run for it but Charlie was too quick for her, he just sidestepped and blocked her path. So, in a state of panic, she took the only option left to her and swung a punch at his belly. Again he was one step ahead of her; he simply grabbed hold of her wrist, spun her around and twisted her arm up her back. Toni squealed in agony. Just then a huge boy appeared from around the corner.

"Oi Porky, let go of her or else I'm going to thump yer onion!" said Michael, taking off his jacket and flexing his muscles.

Charlie immediately let go of Toni and stood quivering and gulping, not sure whether to run or face his new opponent.

"Who are you?"

"My name's Mickey Muscles and I'm going to be giving the orders around here, and I'm going to start by telling you to stop bullying people and pinching their dinner money."

"Oh yeah," said Charlie, slowly regaining some of his composure. "Well, me and the lads think different. In fact we'll have your pocket money off you before you know it, isn't that right lads?"

He turned to his cronies for support only to find that they were all backing away shaking their heads.

"Right, come here. I'm going to give you the biggest wedgie you ever had," said Michael. He then charged at the bully screaming the most terrifying "Roooaaar!" that he could muster.

Chunky Charlie did what all bullies do without the support of their gang. He turned on his heels and fled, squealing like a little piglet. Michael burst into a fit of giggles.

"Thanks Michael, that was very brave of you, but I'm not sure it was wise making an enemy of Charlie so soon. After all you'll have to return to your own size sooner or later won't you?"

"Ooh ek, I'd not thought of that," said Michael, suddenly feeling rather worried about what he'd just done.

"Well, let's worry about that later, for now let's get to lessons before we're late."

Toni led Michael to his classroom, wished him luck and promised to meet him at break time; then she left to join her own class. Michael stood alone outside his classroom. Its door bore a brass plaque with the name "Mr Scrimshaw" written on it. Despite his new size and strength he suddenly felt very afraid and lonely. He took a deep breath and then, with all of his willpower he knocked on the door.

"Come in," came the well-spoken reply from inside the classroom.

Michael turned the doorknob and entered. As he did so, thirty pairs of eyes, including Mr Scrimshaw's turned and stared at him. Every person in the room had their mouths open in shock.

'Just like shoal of guppy fish,' thought Michael. He was beginning to tire of the reaction people were having at the sight of him, and he could feel his face turning scarlet with embarrassment as no one spoke a word. They just continued to ogle at him. Eventually, Mr Scrimshaw regained some self-control and instructed him to sit down.

"I'm afraid you're going to have to sit at the back young man. If you sit at the front anyone sat behind you will only see the back of your head rather than the whiteboard."

At this, one or two of the children giggled behind their hands. Michael made his way to the back of the room, but at first couldn't see any seats available, and then he spotted it, his heart sank even further. All the children were sat two by two and Michael's table mate was a small boy who, it was obvious even at the first glance, was the class 'stinky.' The boy turned to him, his tiny eyes squinting and blinking through extremely thick jam jar spectacles. He patted the empty seat next to him and the rest of the class erupted once more into a fit of hysterics. Michael plonked himself down next to his new chum. The boy said nothing at first; he just continued to peer up at him and looked for all the world like a little mole that had just popped up from the ground. Then he just gave Michael a big warm and somewhat odorous smile, which revealed a mouthful of higgledy-piggledy brown teeth and offered Michael his hand.

"Hello there, my name is Boris, Boris Odbin; pleased to meet you!"

Michael resisted the urge to gag at the smell of Boris's breath and shook his hand.

"Hiya, my name's Michael Moon, pleased to meet you too."

"Can I ask you a question please?"

"Erm, yes Boris, fire away."

"You're not going to thump me are you?"

"No, of course not, why on earth would I do that?"

"Well, everybody else does, and seeing as how you're really big I figured that a thump off of you would really hurt. So let's get this straight right away, there's no point in stamping on my feet, pulling my hair or twisting my ear to get my dinner money because I don't have any. I'm on free school meals."

"Boris, stop worrying, I'm not going to hit you or steal dinner money. I'm not like that. Besides you seem ok to me."

Boris seemed taken aback by this, he was used to people picking on him and calling him names.

"You seem nice too, for a big lad that is, can we be friends then?"

Michael sighed, he knew that befriending Boris would make his own popularity sink even further. But Boris seemed nice and Michael needed all the friends he could get at the moment.

"Yes, I'd like that," replied Michael.

He spent the rest of the lesson banging his knees on the underside of their small table and he noticed that, after being sat for over an hour, he began to stiffen up and his back ached badly. Michael wondered if this is what it was like to be a grown-up like his dad. If so, he wasn't particularly looking forward to growing up.

The day continued to get worse for Michael. His next lesson was music with Mrs White. All the children sat down cross-legged in a circle around the piano and sang along as their teacher played for them, but Michael found that he could no longer sit cross-legged. His legs were too stiff and they simply wouldn't bend like that anymore. He had to sit with them straight out in front of him, which meant that he took up a good chunk of the floor to himself. Michael was really fed up; he hated singing because he couldn't sing in tune or hold a note if his life depended on it. So he tried to sing as quietly as possible, but despite this his deep voice could be heard as a deep drone above all of the other children. This seemed to irritate and amuse the others in equal measure and soon drew the attention of Mrs White. Far from being annoyed by the distraction, Mrs White seemed tickled pink that she had a baritone voice in her choir.

"Oh what a wonderfully rich and deep voice you have young man. Come up here and sing with me."

Michael's heart nearly stopped and he turned the colour of pickled beetroot as he was forced to stand in front of the piano and sing a duet with his teacher. By the time they had sung their way through, 'Kumbaya my Lord', several of the children had literally wet themselves through uncontrollable laughter. Michael had never been so embarrassed in his life; he knew that this was the stuff that legends were made of and that the other kids would remind him of this day for the rest of his school life.

Playtime turned out to be just as disastrous. Toni met up with him as promised and in the hope of cheering him up invited him to play football with her and her friends. Unfortunately, Michael hadn't quite mastered his new size yet, so every time he went in for a tackle he sent the poor recipient sprawling across the playground. Worse still was whenever he did manage to get a shot of the ball, he'd kick it in the usual way but it would leave his foot with the force of a cannonball and send the poor children, including the goalkeeper, ducking for cover. It wasn't long before the boys refused to play if Michael was playing.

"Toni, you idiot, why did you have to invite Goliath along, he's as clumsy as a bull in a china shop."

"Yeah, he stood on my foot, I think he's squashed it flat," said another or Toni's friends.

"And look at the state of my tab where he launched the ball at it. It felt like being kicked in the ear by a donkey," said a little chubby boy pointing at his crimson lughole.

"Yes, get rid of him Toni, or else you're both not playing," said the first boy.

"Hey, come on guys, there's no need to be cruel," protested Toni.

"It's ok, they're right, I'm too big to play, I'll go and find somewhere to sit and watch. I'll see you later."

Michael turned and walked away feeling utterly miserable. He couldn't believe how stupid he'd been to wish that he was big. He'd hoped that being as big as his father would have made his first day at school an easy one, but he couldn't possibly have been more wrong. He made up his mind that his next wish would be to return to his normal size. Michael couldn't wait for the bell to ring to signal the end of his first miserable day at school. When it did, he leapt up, grabbed his bag and coat and ran as fast as he could from the classroom, bowling over children, left, right and centre like tenpin skittles. He tore across the yard in the direction of the main gates where he knew his mum would be waiting in the car ready to whisk him and Toni away to safety. Instead, all he could see was a row of vans and lorries with satellite dishes on their roofs blocking the school gates. Beneath them were several dozen men and women all carrying either microphones or big fluffy sponges on long sticks. Michael could see that it was a television crew, but what could they be doing here he wondered as he made his way toward them. As he approached they seemed to get more and more excited by the second, and then suddenly one young woman shouted out.

"Hello there, you must be Michael Moon? For the benefit of our viewers could you tell me your height and your age please?"

Michael was just about to reply when a young man butted in with another question.

"Did you know that you could possibly be the tallest boy in the world? Have you been in touch with the book of world records? How does this make you feel?"

Michael turned to answer the young man when another reporter asked him a question, and then another and another. The news crews were whipping themselves up into a frenzy of excitement and were crowding in all around him, shoving microphones in his face and clonking him on the head with the sound booms. All the time this was happening, a hundred bright flash bulbs were going off in front of his eyes.

"Why are you so tall?"

"Are your parents really big? Or is it some kind of freak gene?"

Michael was frightened and could feel his eyes filling up with tears. Just what he needed he thought, now everyone was going to see him on TV and think he was a cry baby. He tried to push through the baying crowd, but they wouldn't let him go.

"Do you feel weird being so tall at your age?"

Michael couldn't help himself; he just broke down and started to cry. Just as the reporter was about to open his poisonous mouth and fire another cruel question at him, a large handbag came crashing down on top of his head.

"I'll give you weird, you cheeky bugger, leave my son alone, that goes for the lot of you!"

It was Michael's mum and she was swinging her handbag around like a medieval mace. Once she'd cleared a path through the crowd, she grabbed hold of Michael's arm and led him to the car as quickly as possible, the press pack chasing them all the way. As soon as they were all in the car, his mum sped away from the scene. Michael sat shaking like a leaf and continued to cry for all he was worth. Toni put an arm around him and gave him a hug, which did make him feel a little better. More than anything else he couldn't wait until midnight when he could use his next wish and put everything right.

Chapter Five

Things Get a Little Worse

The rest of the day passed agonisingly slowly. It had seemed like an eternity since he'd got back home from school and Michael couldn't stop himself from glancing impatiently at the clock. He'd sat and watched TV with his parents until eight o' clock, when his dad had instructed him to go to bed. Michael had protested that seeing as he was a big grown-up now, he should be able to stop up until they went to bed too, but his father was having none of it.

"Bed, now and don't forget to brush your teeth"

Once he was in bed, his mum came and read him a bedtime story, she tucked him in and kissed the top of his head, just as she always did, she wished him sweet dreams and left him alone with his night light on. As soon as he heard her footsteps descending the stairs he crept out of bed and across to his portable telly. He switched it on and winced as a horrifyingly loud advert featuring a monkey banging a drum kit, blared out of the TV at full volume. He immediately turned the volume right down and stood, frozen, straining his ears for any signs that his parents had heard what he was up to. After a few minutes had gone by and there were no angry shouts from downstairs, he presumed that he had got away with it this time. He left the volume right down but flicked through the channels until he found something that interested him, and then tiptoed back across the room and climbed back into bed. He lay there watching the TV determined to stay awake; he didn't want to fall asleep and miss the clock ticking past midnight, as far as he was concerned the sooner he could change back to his old self the better. At about half past ten he heard his parents coming up to bed. So he got up and turned the TV off and then curled up under the blankets pretending to be asleep just in case his mum looked in on him, which she did. He listened to them brushing their teeth in the bathroom, after which they went to bed. For a long time he could hear them talking, they were saying how worried they were about him. They said that they would take him to the doctor's tomorrow but they were afraid of what they might say. Then he heard his mum start to cry and his dad trying to comfort her. Michael started to cry too, he couldn't believe how much trouble he'd caused. By the time midnight finally came, he was feeling very tired. He'd never stayed up this late before in his life. His eyes were really sore from all the crying he'd been doing and he was beginning to get a headache. He kicked off the bed clothes and climbed out of bed. The only light in the room came from the glowing red numbers on his bedside alarm clock. His mum had turned off the night light when she had looked in on him and he hadn't dared put it back on again in case they had noticed the light shining through the gap at the bottom of the door. Michael groped his way across the room to where the cauldron was sat, quiet and lifeless. He'd been waiting for this moment all day but now the time had come he found that he was very afraid. The house seemed so different at this time of night; everything seemed so quiet and dark. Images of monsters crawling out from under the bed or zombies, bandaged arms outstretched, approaching him through the darkness, began to fill his head. Michael quickly opened the blinds to let some moonlight in. He looked down at the big black silhouette of the cauldron on his desk and noticed the moon's reflection on the water. He opened his mouth to make his wish but, before he'd even had the chance to speak, the moon's reflection broke up as the water in the pot began to ripple and dance with excitement. It was as if it could sense his presence and knew he was about to make a wish. Michael was beginning to have serious doubts about the cauldron, it seemed mischievous and untrustworthy, but never the less, if he didn't want to spend the rest of his days as a giant boy he was going to have to make his wish.

'Here goes,' he thought to himself. He took a deep breath and then spoke, quietly but clearly.

"I want to go back to being normal, it's horrible being big; I wish that I was little."

Once again the contents of the pot began to bubble and fizz violently and the fluid turned to a vivid scarlet. The little white letters appeared on the surface and floated about until they formed a sentence.

"Your wish is granted." He watched as the fluid then returned to the natural translucent appearance of water and the moon's reflection gradually reformed as the surface calmed itself. For a few minutes nothing happened, which made Michael begin to panic. What happens if the cauldron had stopped working and couldn't grant him his wish, he'd be stuck this way forever. He could feel the fear rising up inside of him and was on the verge of crying again when all of a sudden he felt the pyjamas that his father had given him begin to grow. His arms began retracting up the sleeves, his PJ bottoms fell down around his ankles and his head started to disappear into the neck hole of his top. 'This is it' he thought, a sense of relief flooding over him. He watched as the window, which only moments ago had been at head height, slowly appeared to climb the wall and was now towering above him. It felt like he was in an elevator with a glass door and was watching the world go up as he was plummeting down and down, in fact too far down. He felt sure that he hadn't been this small before. Only a day and a half ago, he'd brought the cauldron home and placed it on his desk and although it did seem a long time ago and many things had happened since then, he could clearly remember standing on tiptoe and staring down at the contents of the pot. Now the cauldron was well above his eye line in fact he wasn't even as tall as his desk.

'What's going on?' thought Michael, the panic inside of him immediately returning. He didn't want this; he said he wanted to be normal again. Then suddenly, realisation came upon him like a hammer blow.

He'd said, "I want to go back to being normal, it's horrible being big, I wish I was little."

And little is exactly what he was rapidly becoming.

"Oh, no, no, no, no, no," shouted Michael at the top of his voice but the sound that came out of him was no louder than the squeak of a tiny mouse.

He continued to shrink, smaller and smaller. He was now so little that he had completely disappeared into his dad's pyjamas and it felt like he was inside a huge wedding tent that had collapsed on top of him. He shouted for help as loudly as he could but his tiny squeaks fell on deaf ears. He tried desperately to find a way out, crawling this way and that amongst the folds of material until eventually a dim chink of light led him out of one of the sleeve's cuffs. He rolled out on to the carpet and stood up. It appeared that he'd stopped shrinking but now he stood no taller than his mobile phone. Michael stood naked and shivering in the cold night air. Now he really was in a pickle, at least last time he'd been able to borrow his dad's clothes, what on earth was he going to do this time. He looked around helplessly at the alien world he now found himself in. His toy cars were now just about big enough for him to climb inside, his dad's shoes, which still lay in the middle of the floor, where he'd kicked them off, looked like two beached whales and worst of all if he wanted to use the TV controller, he was going to have to climb up on to it and jump up and down on the buttons. He was well and truly stuffed, he'd already tried shouting for help but to no avail, he couldn't just go and get help because the door's handle was now miles above his head and, even if the door had been left ajar, it would be far too heavy for him to move. He couldn't even climb into bed to keep warm as the top of the mattress was now the height of a three-storey building. He thought of climbing the bedsheets that hung down to the floor but decided against it as a fall from that height would probably do him serious harm. His only option was to use one of his old socks as a sleeping bag. It would probably be a bit smelly but seeing as he was covered in goosebumps and his teeth were chattering like castanets, it was a sacrifice he was prepared to make. Once inside his cheesy new bed, he quickly warmed up and, despite the smell, it wasn't long before sleep was upon him. He was so tired that he slept soundly all night until he was woken by the all too familiar call of the alarm clock. Michael popped his head out of his sock and looked up to where his alarm clock sat, high above him on his bedside drawers. He realised that he wasn't going to be able to turn it off and wondered how long it would continue to beep before it drew the attention of his parents. Sure enough, after a couple of minutes his mum shouted up to him.

"Michael, come on, get up and switch that clock off."

When she didn't get a reply, she came charging up the stairs in a less than jovial mood and the sound of her rapidly approaching footsteps made a series of terrifying thoughts suddenly occur to Michael. What if his mum came bursting into his room only to find an empty bed then ran off in a panic, shutting the door behind her and trapping him in again or even worse, maybe she would come galloping in, not see him down here on the floor and tread on him. He'd end up as flat as a pancake. He scrambled out of his sock and bolted across the bedroom floor to take shelter under the corner of his desk.

"Michael, are you deaf? Switch that thing off and get up." No reply came. "I'm going to count to three and then I'm coming in, and boy will you be in trouble." Still no reply, "One, two, three, right that's it, I'm coming in and I'm going to slap your bottom, I don't care how big you are."

He watched as an angry, red-faced version of his mum came bursting into his room. She thundered straight across to the alarm clock and turned it off with a furious thump of her fist. She then turned and whipped the bedsheets back, fully expecting to find her son fast asleep but instead found an empty bed. She stood there for a moment or two in surprised silence wondering where he might have gone, so Michael took this opportunity to shout to her. At first she didn't hear him, so he tried a second time and he watched as her head turned this way and that, trying to locate where the sound was coming from. He tried again shouting for all he was worth and this time it worked. Her head snapped around in his direction and her gaze fell directly upon him. He was fully expecting a repeat performance of the goldfish routine but what she did this time was far more frightening. She clutched at her hair with both hands and let out the most blood-curdling scream he'd ever heard, her face contorted into a picture of pure terror.

"Mum, it's me, Michael, please don't be frightened," he pleaded.

He ran out from under the desk, arms open wide in the hope that she'd pick him up but she just leapt up on to his bed and backed away as far as she could, the way she often did when she'd seen a spider. She just continued to scream and scream and Michael pleaded with her to come down and help him but she just leapt off the bed and fled from the room as fast as she could go. Michael made to follow her but when he heard his dad bounding up the stairs he once more retreated to the shelter of his desk.

"Emma, what on earth is going on, are you ok?" He heard his dad go into his parents' bedroom and then an almighty argument broke out as he tried to calm his hysterical wife.

"I think all the pressure of the last few days is beginning to take its toll on you; perhaps you should see the doc. today as well."

"How dare you, there's nothing wrong with my sanity, if you don't believe me just go in there and take a look for yourself."

"Ok, I will, if only to put your mind at rest and show you that he's ok."

Michael watched as his dad came into the room and looked all around him for any signs of his son.

"He's not even here, are you sure he's not gone around to call for Toni?"

Immediately, Michael's mum appeared at his shoulder and quickly found Michael cowering under the corner of the desk. She shrieked again and pointed to where he stood.

"Now tell me I'm seeing things."

His dad looked to where she was indicating and the colour completely vanished from his face, he sank to his knees and put his head in his hands.

"I'm losing my mind, I can't bare this. I'm losing my mind." He said over and over again as he rocked backward and forward and began to sob.

"You can't be, we can both see that he's shrunk, so it's got to be some kind of voodoo or witchcraft or something," said his mum as she too dropped to her knees and put her arms around her husband to comfort him.

Things were going from bad to worse for Michael. The rest of the world thought that he was some kind of giant freak, his mum and dad thought that he'd been cursed and were terrified of him and, worst of all, he was now so tiny that doing all the things that he loved would no longer be possible, in fact just surviving the day in this giant world would be extremely difficult. Michael decided that now was the time to own up and tell his parents about the cauldron, at least then they might be able to understand what was going on. He stepped out from his shelter and timidly made his way across to where his mum and dad were knelt. At first they began to back away and covered their ears when he tried to speak to them but when he fell to his knees and put his hands together as if in prayer and begged them to listen, they took pity on him. They sat in stunned silence as Michael recounted the whole story of the magic cauldron. His father just nodded occasionally and appeared to be thinking very carefully about what was being said. His mum was less convinced though.

"Really Michael, what do you take us for, magic cauldrons that grant people wishes, that's the stuff of fairy tales."

"Usually I'd agree with you Emma but seeing as our son has gone from being four foot, to six foot and is currently stood before us measuring no more than four inches high, I'm inclined to believe him."

Michael was a little surprised by this turn of events as it was usually his mum that sided with him, whilst Dad stuck to his guns.

"I'm telling the truth, Mum, please believe me."

"No, no I'm having none of this, magic cauldrons! Pah rubbish, look I'll show you it's nothing more than an old cooking pot."

Michael was about to warn her that only he could make the wishes but she didn't give him the chance, she marched straight over to his desk, grabbed the cauldron with both hands and shouted very loudly.

"I wish that my son was back to his normal self again."

But instead of the cauldron granting her a wish, it just made the loudest belching noise he'd ever heard and at the same time emitted an eggy green cloud of vapour that enveloped his mum's head. She immediately dropped the cauldron and began to gag.

"Pooh, heck, what on earth is that smell, it reminds me of the time when the drains exploded," she said amidst coughs and splutters and she looked at him through watering eyes.

Michael resisted the urge to laugh and could see that Dad too, was having to keep himself in check.

"Mum, I've already told you, it has to be me that makes the wishes."

His mum said nothing; she just stood nervously surveying the cauldron.

"What happens to the cauldron when you have made your final wish? Does it become free to grant wishes to a new owner?" said his dad, with a look of curiosity and greed beginning to spread across his face.

"I suppose so, why do you ask?" said Michael suspiciously.

"Well, I was thinking that when we have got you back to your old self, maybe I could be the next to have a go with it. Just think of all the possibilities, we could be rich, we could retire and spend the rest of our lives on holiday, ooh and what about that new sports car that I've always wanted, mmmmm."

That was it, he'd lost his father, there was no point in trying to dissuade him, his face had got that gormless, dreamy look about it. Michael turned to his mum in the hope of getting some good old-fashioned common sense but she too had envy and greedy lust written all over her face.

"Ooh yeh, just think of all the shoes and dresses. I could have luxury weekends at a spa being pampered and a personal trainer called Enrique or something."

"Oi, stop that and roll your tongue back in, there'll be no Enreaky or whatever you call him, there's only four wishes and I want me flippin' sports car, I've always wanted one, in red I think."

"You selfish sod, do you mean to tell me that you'd have all the wishes for yourself?"

"Yes, they're mine; besides, you could have the cauldron when I've finished with it."

"Ooh yeh, I'd not thought of that," said his mum, the soppy expression quickly returning to her face.

"HEY, KNOCK IT OFF, the pair of you," squeaked Michael as loudly as he could.

"The cauldron is really dangerous, if you don't make your wish with the correct wording all sorts can go wrong, just look at you two now, you're squabbling like a pair of kids at infant school."

Sadly it was too late. Michael's pleas fell on deaf ears. The green monster of greed had already taken them.

"You can't keep it you know, you've nearly had your turn, and thanks for the warning but you needn't be concerned, I'll make sure I make my wish properly," said his dad, sounding more like a spoilt brat than a supposedly responsible adult.

"Right, let's go and get some breakfast, all this excitement has given me an appetite," said Mum.

His parents got up and made for the door, grinning from ear to ear like a pair of Cheshire cats.

"Hey, what about me I'd like some breakfast too, I'm starving and it would take me half of the day to get downstairs."

"Oh, sorry Michael," said his mum as she bent down and placed him in the palm of her hand.

"I don't know what we're going to give you for your breakfast; I don't think that I can slice toast that small. More importantly, what are we going to dress you in, we can't have you walking around in your birthday suit all day, can we?"

Michael blushed scarlet.

"We could always use that old sock of his, if we nick a few holes in it for his arms and legs to go through, he'd be as snug as a bug in a rug."

"No way, Dad that would look so dumb, besides I've already used it as a sleeping bag and it smells really cheesy."

His dad started to laugh.

"Well that will teach you to get a bath a little more often, wont it?"

"Ha ha, very funny, Dad," said Michael, looking to his mum for help.

"Tell him please, I can't wear that."

"Stop teasing him Steven, you know damn well we can't have our son walking around dressed in an old sock, what would thc neighbours think?"

"There, that told you, Dad," said Michael, blobbing out his tongue.

"What am I going to wear, Mum?"

"Hmmm, well the only thing that I can think of is that teddy that we bought Kizzy for her birthday, it's about the same size as you and I'm sure its clothes would fit nicely."

Michael nearly fainted when he realised which teddy in particular his mum was referring to.

"No way, you can't possibly mean Boo Boo the monkey, can you Mum?"

"Yes, why not, they're perfectly good clothes."

"Perfectly good clothes; Mum, he wears bright pink shorts that are held up with braces and a pink T-shirt that says, 'I love snuggles'. I couldn't possibly wear them, I'd rather die."

"Yes, that's precisely what I'm afraid of, if we don't put you something on, you'll catch your death of cold, so I'm afraid that it's either Boo Boo's clothes or your cheesy sock, which is it to be young man?"

Michael sat and pondered the question for a moment or two; it was like being torn between the devil and the deep blue sea. On the one hand he was going to have to walk around all day encased in an uncomfortable old sock that smelt like a bag of cheese and onion crisps or, on the other, he was going to have to suffer the ignominy of having to wear Boo Boo's bright pink hand-me-down shorts. Eventually he plumped for Boo Boo's outfit. His mum went in to Kizzy's bedroom and stripped her teddy of its clothes; she then handed them to Michael and waited whilst he got dressed. Once he'd finished, Michael glumly inspected his reflection in the mirror. Standing there resplendent in his new powder pink get up, he resembled a really silly children's TV presenter. Michael's mum picked him up and carried him downstairs. Once in the kitchen, she plonked him on the table and left him there whilst she went to attend to the breakfast. Kizzy, who was brandishing a teaspoon as if it were Thor's hammer, had been busy sploshing her mushy Weetabix around the kitchen but stopped immediately when she saw Michael peeping at her from behind the salt pot. She dropped her spoon and stared at him with intense curiosity. He didn't dare approach her for fear of that she might do. Babies were clumsy and, compared to him, she was now the size of an elephant. If she were to fling her arms around and knock him off the table, the fall would certainly kill him and a bonk on the head from her teaspoon wouldn't do him a power of good either. Just then his mum dropped the knife that she'd been spreading the toast with on to the metal draining board. The clatter made him jump and spin around to see what was going on. He was just about to curse his mum for giving him a fright, when all of a sudden a big clammy hand encased him and plucked him from his hiding place. It was Kizzy, she'd reached over and snatched him up in her pudgy fist and was now holding him up, eye to eye. She tilted her head to one side, the expression on her face blank as she appeared to be trying to work something out. It suddenly dawned on Michael that any number of terrifying scenarios might take place from this moment onwards and, sure enough, Kizzy's face crinkled up into a big broad smile and she squeaked with delight.

"BOO, BOO."

She then gave him a playful squeeze with a force that was out of this world. It was horrendous. He felt like he was inside an industrial press. The pressure in his head made both of his ears go 'pop' and his eyes bulged out of their sockets. He opened his mouth to scream but couldn't as all the air had been expelled from his lungs; just when he though that he couldn't take any more, Kizzy released her grip. He gasped for air as his not-so-little sister stared at him with a deep frown etched upon her face.

"Boo, Boo's squeaker not working."

Next, Kizzy did what all infants do when they're faced with an object that they can't figure out; she shoved him into her mouth. Michael's eyes lit up in terror as his head and shoulders entered the big pink smelly chasm. Half-formed baby teeth, covered in soggy cereal, flashed past either side of his face, and as he was pushed further in, a big pair of red tonsils, the size of water melons, loomed into view.

"Aaaaahh!" screamed Michael.

It was like being forced through the gates of hell. Just as he was beginning to think that all was lost and was bracing himself for the inevitable shark-powered bite from Kizzy's baby stumps, he suddenly found himself being catapulted backward as Kizzy spat him out with a disgusted "Pah."

He landed on the table with a bump, covered from head to foot in goo and half-masticated Weetabix. Michael got up and shook his fist at her, he was furious with his little sister.

"What's the matter with you, are you blind or something? That was disgusting; if I wasn't so little, I'd come over there and wallop you, I swear I would."

Far from being cowed by Michael's chastising, Kizzy became more excited than ever.

"Iky Meeky Moo."

The prospect of her brother becoming her pocket-sized playmate filled her with joy and she sprang forwards, making a grab for him. Michael leapt backwards and scurried across the table out of harm's way. Kizzy burst into tears and roared for all she was worth until her mum came over to see what was wrong.

"Want pway with iky Meeky Moo."

"Oh no, I don't think that would be wise, here have your dum dum instead."

With that, her mum hammered home the pacifier like a cork into a barrel of beer. Michael breathed a sigh of relief as he glanced over to where hid dad was sitting. It appeared that Pops had claimed himself a new chair and, as always, sat obscured from view by the morning paper. Under normal circumstances he would be mumbling and tutting at various articles before launching into a five minute rant about the price of petrol and the ever increasing size of potholes, but today he just whistled and hummed merrily. It was nice to see him happy again, he'd been down in the dumps and depressed for a while. He'd been worried about leaving his job in town and moving to the country at such short notice, but now something had brightened his mood and Michael could guess what it was. He dreaded what was going to happen to his family when his dad got hold of the magic cauldron and moments later his concerns were justified when his father spoke.

"Do you know what I'm going to do today?"

"Hmmm," replied Mum, not really listening.

"I'm going to ring in sick and have the day off of work, then I'm going in to town and I'm going to buy that great big TV that we were saying that we liked, after that I'm going to treat myself to a new mobile phone, some new clothes, a new coat and I'm going to buy you those revolting shoes that you were pestering for."

"Ooooh Steven, thank you," said Mum, clapping her hands together like an excited schoolgirl.

"But Dad, every time I've asked for something new recently, you've just told me that we can't afford it because of the procession."

"I think you mean recession and, no, we can't afford these things, so I'm going to put everything on my credit cards and pay them off with all the money I'm going to make from that cauldron."

Michael didn't really understand any of this but he wasn't sure he liked the sound of it. He felt really miserable, he could see that trouble was brewing on the horizon and it was all his fault and, what was worse, he had no one to turn to for help. His parents had both been seduced by the powers of the cauldron, Kizzy was too young to understand and even his best friend Toni would be powerless to help. Then a thought suddenly struck. Maybe Toni's dad could help, he'd had dealings with the cauldron before, or at least that was what old Elsie from the shop was alluding to. Hopefully, he would know a way to get out of this mess before things got even worse. Michael seriously hoped so, but first he was going to have to work out a way of getting down safely from the table and crossing the floor without getting squished and then somehow make his way through one of the doors, which he could no longer open.

Michael sat in the middle of a saucer chewing on a postage stamp-sized piece of toast and pondered his options. As he looked around the room in search of a safe escape route, he happened to notice the picture on the front page of the newspaper that his dad was reading. It was of his mum, frozen in time with her arm held aloft, brandishing a handbag that was poised, ready to come down on the hapless reporter's head. She'd been snapped pulling the most comical face Michael had ever seen which made him burst out laughing and nearly choke on his toast crumbs. His mum turned in his direction to see what all the fuss was about and that was when she too spotted the front page.

"Good grief, is that me on the front of your paper?"

"Erm, no dear, it's ehem er, somebody else altogether," said his dad as he tried to fold the paper backwards to obscure her view of the front page.

"Yes it is, let me have a look."

"No, really, it's nothing; you wouldn't be interested I can assure you."

He protested and held the paper up above his head so that she couldn't reach it. His mum was having none of it though. She didn't bother trying to reach up and snatch it; she simply grabbed hold of his right ear and twisted it with all of her might.

"OUCH!" screamed Dad, as he dropped the paper and cupped his hand over his pulsating earhole. Mum picked up the paper and immediately turned to the front page.

"'Giant boy's mum goes ga, ga', I don't believe it, Steven have you seen this, the cheeky swines."

"Oooh I'm going out," said Dad as he got up from the table and marched over to the sink to wash his breakfast bowl.

"Grrrr, this is unbelievable, the lies that they've written about me, what will the neighbours say and as for that photo, I refuse to believe I look like that, they've definitely altered that on the computer or something."

"Oh I don't know, I thought it was a good likeness, in fact I was thinking of putting it on the mantelpiece to scare Kizzy away from the fire," mumbled Dad under his breath, thinking that he couldn't be heard.

Unfortunately Mum's hearing was better than radar and she picked up every word that he said.

"Oi, I heard that, saucy," said Mum as she picked up Kizzy's empty plastic cup and hurled it across the room at him.

It hit him on the back of the head with a mighty loud CLOMP. Furious, he spun around ready to give his wife a piece of his mind just in time to catch the second plastic mug right in the middle of the forehead. CLOMP. Michael's dad turned purple with rage and, despite the fact that there were children present, he started hurling some very fruity language in the direction of his mum. Amusing as all of this was, Michael decided that now was the time to make his escape whilst his parents were distracted. He sprinted across the table to its edge and leapt the gap to the back of the chair on which his father's coat was hanging. The jump was far greater than he'd anticipated and he began to fall short. Instead of landing on the top of the chair back, he slammed into it with his chest, knocking the wind out of him. He just managed to grab hold of the top in time to save himself from a disastrous fall. Michael just dangled, hanging on for all he was worth until he caught his breath back, then he pulled himself up and stood on top of the chair back. He stretched his arms out either side of himself and tiptoed across the narrow edge like a tightrope walker, his task made even harder by the fact that his father's coat was made from suede and was very slippery under foot. Once he reached the end of the chair, he slid down the coat's sleeve like a fireman's pole until he reached the cuff and then let go, dropping the short distance to the ground. Michael was panting but there was no time to rest. His parents' argument was fizzling out and, instead of standing and shouting at one another, they were starting to move around the kitchen. He ran and hid behind one of the tree trunk sized table legs and watched his father's huge feet approach the table. He saw his dad remove his coat from the chair back and then he pushed the chair under with a horrifyingly loud squeak.

"Right, I'm going out now love, I'll see you later, I won't be long," said Dad as he turned to make his way to the door.

Michael suddenly realised that this was going to be his best chance of getting through the front door. He decided that he wasn't going to try to run through the door as hid dad opened it – that would be far too dangerous; he'd either be spotted or, worse still, if he got his timing wrong, he'd be squished in the door frame. His best bet would be to hitch a ride on his dad's trouser leg or his shoe. Whichever he decided to do, he would have to do it quickly as his dad was already halfway to the back door. In reality his dad was only sauntering along but to Michael he was moving away from him faster than an Olympic sprinter. He set off in pursuit as fast as his little legs would carry him and only caught up when his dad paused to open the front door. Michael leapt the last bit and landed on top of his dad's shoe. He let his legs dangle either side of his dad's foot and grabbed hold of the laces for safety. His dad closed the door behind himself and set off at a brisk pace toward the garage. The ride turned out to be the most uncomfortable he'd ever taken and, as his dad's foot went up and down, backwards and forwards, he began to feel like a cowboy riding the rodeo. He was relieved when they finally reached the garage and his dad stopped to let himself in. Michael leapt clear of his dad's feet and scuttled across the gravel drive out of harm's way. Moments later, he heard the car's engine spring into life with a mighty roar that made the ground beneath his little feet tremble. He watched as the car slowly emerged from the garage and then he was forced to duck for cover when pieces of gravel as big as beach balls were fired at him as the car accelerated quickly away. Michael gave a huge sigh, if he'd thought that being a giant schoolboy had been troublesome enough then today was turning out to be ten times worse. He was going to have to hope with all of his heart that Toni's dad could help him because with only one more wish remaining, he couldn't afford to make any more mistakes.

Chapter Six

Hiding in the Whistling Tree

Michael crouched down behind the two enormous milk bottles witch stood outside the front door of Vixen Cottage. He was taking a minute or two to catch his breath after the climb up the garden's stone steps. He was beginning to get annoyed at how much time and effort even the smallest of tasks was requiring to complete. Michael studied the huge wooden door. At its very top was the number seven, which Michael thought was odd seeing as there were only four houses on Foxwood Lane and none of the others were numbered, they all had names instead. Underneath the number were two long stained glass panels. The one on the left depicted an old man with a long white beard and a staff who looked very much like many of the wizards Michael had seen in his story books. The panel on the right was a scene of a king in his suit of arms, holding a shield bearing his royal crest. He proudly stood in front of a very grand medieval castle and when Michael looked more closely, he could see that it was the castle from the hilltop, before it had been crumbled by the hands of time. He wondered what story the pictures were trying to tell him and if the old man in the first scene was Toni's dad, because he did bare a strong resemblance to him. Just then a gust of wind rattled the cat flap at the bottom of the door and brought him back to his senses. He'd not noticed it before now but was very pleased to see it, as it made the job of getting into the house so much easier. On the downside though, it meant that there would almost certainly be a cat hanging around somewhere. This meant that if he didn't want to end up as breakfast for a hippopotamus-sized feline, then he was going to have to tread very carefully indeed. After five minutes of huffing, puffing and pushing, Michael finally managed to enter the house through the cat flap. He quickly scanned the room for an escape route, should a hungry moggy appear. Fortunately there was no sign of a cat or anybody else for that matter. As Michael made his way across the stone flagged floor, he was struck once again by how much ancient looking clutter there was in the house. The pictures, the books, the rolls of parchment with drawings of strange contraptions on them, and the little brass lamp with its incense candle that burned away slowly on the mantelpiece. They gave the house an eerie, old world feel that intrigued and excited him greatly. He wondered what Toni's dad did for a living. Perhaps he was a history teacher or a scientist or something. Michael continued his journey across the lounge, passing old leather sofas as he made his way toward the door into the kitchen. On his right was a bookshelf full of old leather-bound books. The bottom shelf was low enough for him to be able to read the titles of the books, which were written in gold letters on the books' spines. They were all old scientific books, such as *Medicine in the dark ages*, *The physician's handbook* and *Ancient potion making*. He continued to read as he made his way to the end of the shelf. Just as he read the last title, something in the corner of his vision made him stop and freeze. There was something stood in the doorway into the kitchen. His worst fears had come true, for when he turned to face the object, he saw an old grey and white tabby cat glaring back at him. His heart hammered wildly in his chest and his muscles refused to move, he was rooted to the spot. Seconds passed as he waited for the cat to make its move and come in for the kill, but thankfully it never happened. Rather than it pace up and down, licking its lips in readiness to pounce, the cat simply stared at him intensely. Its gaze pierced him and he got the distinct impression that it was trying to figure something out. It was a gaze that Michael felt sure he'd seen somewhere before. Eventually the old cat got up and sloped off back into the kitchen and out of sight. Michael heaved a huge sigh of relief.

Today must be his lucky day, he thought, for he'd been certain that once the cat had seen him, it would have mistaken him for a mouse and eaten him. Just then Toni's dad appeared from around the kitchen door and immediately Michael's fear returned. He was out in the open, right in the middle of the floor, with no objects close by that he might take cover under. At any moment he could be trampled to death by the fluffy tartan slippers of the old man, but he needn't have worried, the moment he entered the room, the old man's gaze fell instantly upon him. It was almost as if he'd been expecting to see him there. Once again, to Michael's amazement, Toni's dad didn't seem the slightest bit shocked or surprised at being confronted by a boy the size of a salt pot. He just smiled, creakily got to his knees and then offered Michael his hand to climb into. Michael hesitated, the last time he'd been in someone's hand it had been Kizzy's and she'd squeezed him so hard his eyes had nearly popped out of his head, it was an experience he was rather keen not to repeat. Eventually he decided to trust him and climbed up into his palm. Michael was carefully lifted up and taken into the kitchen, where he was gently placed on the table. The old fella then drew out a chair and sat himself down opposite Michael. At first he said nothing and Michael began to wonder if he was in trouble but then a big grin spread across his lined face and he began to chuckle, heartily.

"Now then young Meeky, it looks like you've been having a LITTLE adventure, come on, I'm dying to know, what have you been up to?"

"Well, erm, it's like this, I'm not making this up, honestly but, erm."

"No, no, don't tell me, let me guess, either your mum has put you and your clothes on a hot wash and shrunk you both or you've come across something that I haven't seen for years and quite frankly had hoped I'd never see again. I'm guessing that you've found the magic cauldron."

Michael was elated, Toni's dad knew about the cauldron, which meant that he could help him get out of the terrible mess he found himself in.

"So it's true then, sir, you do know all about the magic cauldron."

"Well, I wouldn't say that I know everything there is to know about it but I have had dealings with it in the past and I'm afraid to say that they didn't go well."

Michael felt worried, he wasn't sure he wanted to hear any more bad news connected to the cauldron.

"Can I ask you Michael, how you came to know that I'd been involved with the cauldron."

"Erm, yes, it was old Elsie from the shop, she said…"

"Ah, say no more," said Toni's dad, cutting Michael off, midsentence.

"I'm afraid that doesn't surprise me one little bit, Old Elsie Arkwright does love a good bit of gossip and she won't let little things like truth and fact stop her from broadcasting it all over the village, but on this particular occasion, I will admit that she does have her facts right, I did once own the magic cauldron."

"Brilliant, I'm so glad, do you think that you could help me please sir, I've got myself into a right old pickle and I've only got one wish left to sort it all out, if I get this one wrong, I'll be doomed forever."

The old man gave Michael the kindest of smiles.

"Yes, I can see that you're having a LITTLE trouble." He chuckled.

"Of course I'll help you, in any way that I can and please, there's no need to keep calling me sir, my name is Harry."

"Thank you sir, I mean Harry, you're very kind."

"You're most welcome young man," said Harry brushing the compliment aside with a wave of his hand.

"You know, you and I have a lot in common, Michael, we've both fallen prey to that damn cauldron and its wicked tricks, and in my case, I ran out of wishes before I could correct my mistakes, it cost me dearly I can tell you."

For a moment Harry said nothing, he just stared into space and his face that was only moments ago a picture of happiness, turned to one of the deepest sorrow, as he recalled a painful memory.

"I'm afraid it's been playing its devilish games for several centuries now and I'm sure that its creator would have been overjoyed by the chaos and misery that it has caused numerous generations of families from this tiny village."

"Ah, I see," said Michael, the penny finally dropping.

"Is that why the folk from around here don't even seem surprised when they see me looking like a giant one day and a pixie the next."

"That's right, anyone that has lived here for any length of time will be able to tell you all sorts of stories, like the one about old Eric, who wished to be invisible for a day, only to be flattened by the number nine bus, or there was the tale of little Tommy tin ribs. He got so fed up with being picked on by the village bully, Nasty Norbet, that he used one of his wishes on him. Poor old Norbet awoke the next morning to find that he had a head the size of a Space Hopper. Unfortunately for him, Tommy hadn't realised that it was his last wish he was using, so Norbet has been stuck that way ever since then."

"That's awful, I feel really sorry for him," said Michael, trying not to laugh.

"Well don't, it cured him of his horrible bullying ways and besides he says that, once he got used to it, he actually quite likes being that way, he says it makes him feel distinctive and what's more, he always wins first prize at the pub's annual fancy dress party, his impression of a lollipop just has to be seen to be believed."

At this Michael could contain himself no longer; he burst into a fit of giggles.

"No way, that can't have happened, you're having me on."

"I can assure you, young Meeky, that it's all true," said Harry, the twinkle back in his eyes.

"There's been old men and women that have wished that they were younger again but failed to specify how young they wished to be. So as a consequence, the next day they awoke to find themselves in nappies and baby grows."

"That's it, that's exactly what happened to me, every time I make a wish it goes wrong and that's how I've ended up like this. Did something like this happen to you, Harry?"

The old man just gave a sigh.

"No, not quite, I suppose I'd better start from the beginning hadn't I, but it's rather a long story so I'll make us both a nice cup of tea to be going on with, I think I've got a thimble somewhere that you can use as a cup."

Michael watched Harry as he shuffled around the kitchen making tea and realised how much he'd grown to like him already. He was a kind man and Michael felt that he was someone who he could look up to and trust, it almost felt like Harry could be his granddad.

Finally, Harry returned with a huge pot of steaming tea. He poured himself a cup and gave Michael a thimble full, which to him was the size of a window cleaner's bucket.

"Do you take sugar young man?"

"Yes please."

"Well how many is it to be then, hmm, one grain of sugar or two?" chuckled Harry as he tried to extract a tiny portion of sugar with his spoon. Michael laughed too; it was ridiculous how difficult everything was in his new tiny lifestyle. Once they both had their drinks in front of them, Michael sat down crossed-legged and waited patiently for Harry to start his story.

"Well, I suppose it all started on that hot summer afternoon, many years ago. I'd returned home from work and had been asked by my wife if…"

But that's as far as he got, Harry stopped speaking when they heard the rapid, thump, thump, thump, of Toni's footsteps descending the stairs. She burst into the kitchen, ran across the room and gave her dad a kiss on the cheek.

"Morning Dad, did I hear you talking to someone on the telephone."

"No, I was talking to our guest here."

Toni gave him a puzzled look and then glanced around the kitchen in search of the mystery guest.

"Are you feeling alright Dad, you have been remembering to take your pills, haven't you?"

This made Michael giggle and Toni's head turned left and right as she searched for the source of the noise.

"Yes I have been taking my pills, thank you very much young lady. As I said I was talking to our LITTLE friend from next door," said Harry, gesturing toward Michael with a nod of his head. Toni looked in the direction he was indicating. She gave a squeak and clapped her hand over her mouth in surprise.

"Hiya," said Michael with a big cheesy grin on his face.

"No prizes for guessing what you've been up to," said Toni, her face twitching in an effort not to laugh.

"By the way, love your outfit, pink really suits you."

"Grrrr, get stuffed," said Michael, instantly taking offence.

"Aw, look at the little man, he's so cute when he's angry, come and let me snuggle you."

With that Toni shot forward and grabbed hold of him with one hand and ruffled his hair with the other.

"Geroff me, you overgrown pillock, or I'll…"

"You'll what, hmm, knock my block off, well go on then, give it your best shot," said Toni, teasingly.

"Toni, stop tormenting the poor lad or I'll tell him what happened last night after you'd had that second helping of beans on toast."

Toni turned bright red and Michael just stuck his tongue out and blew a raspberry at her. Just then the phone rang; it was Michael's mum enquiring if her missing son had turned up around here. Harry reassured her that he was here and that he was ok, he also offered to look after him for the morning. Michael's mum accepted gratefully and told him she would still give Toni a lift to school. So once she had eaten her breakfast and given Dad a cuddle, Toni stomped off to school, rather sulkily. She didn't really think that it was fair that she had to go whilst Michael got to stay at home but as her dad said, Michael would never make it through the day without being lost or squashed. Harry watched through the window of the living room as Toni walked down the garden path and through the front gate. He then returned to his seat in the kitchen opposite Michael.

"Right I'm sorry about that, I'll get back to my story, where was I?"

"Why did you stop telling the story when Toni came downstairs, doesn't she know the story of the cauldron?"

"No lad, she doesn't, I've never had the courage to tell her, you see there are aspects of the story that might upset her and I fear that she might not want to know me anymore once she knows what I've done."

Michael wasn't sure he liked the sound of this but curiosity got the better of him and he asked Harry to continue with his story.

"Right, ok, where did I get to? oh yes, I'd returned home from work and my wife had asked me if…"

Again Harry was interrupted, this time by Michael.

"I didn't know that you had a wife."

"Oh yes, many years ago."

"But I haven't seen her yet, does she go to work really early or something?"

"No, no, nothing like that," chuckled Harry.

"If you would permit me to continue, all will be explained."

"Ok, sorry."

"I'd returned home from work and my wife had asked me if I'd go out and find our son, Tony, and fetch him in for his tea."

Michael opened his mouth to speak but Harry just shushed him by putting a finger to his lips.

"I knew exactly where I'd find him; he'd almost certainly be playing in the woods at the back of the garden." Harry smiled at Michael.

"Kids love those woods, there's so much to do and explore. There's the rope swing, the bridge, the rocking stone and the secret chute."

Michael's eyes lit up when he heard this.

"Woa, wicked, what's the rocking stone and the secret chute?"

"Harry looked as excited as Michael; he was obviously just getting into his stride and was enjoying telling the story every bit as much as Michael was enjoying listening to it.

"That's a story that Toni can entertain you with another time my lad. Anyway I'd checked all of the locations I've just mentioned and my son was to be found at none of them, so I knew for certain that he'd be playing at the whistling tree."

Harry paused for a second and gave Michael the chance to ask the obvious question.

"The whistling tree is to be found right at the very centre of the woods, it's an old oak tree that has many low branches that children love to climb on; it also has several hollows in its trunk that form the shape of an old woman's face, whose mouth is all puckered up ready to whistle."

"Wow, that's so cool."

"Yes it is rather and what's more, when the wind blows the tree actually does whistle. Anyway as I said, the afternoon was very warm indeed and by the time I'd made my way up to the whistling tree, I was feeling quite hot and bothered, even more so when I didn't immediately see my son playing there. I looked up and scanned the branches for any sign of him, to no avail and then I started checking the hollows in the trunk, as I knew that they were his favourite place in a game of hide and seek. I found nothing in the first two but when I popped my head into the third, the witch's mouth, I came face to face not with my son but a huge copper pot. At first I considered how such an item as this could have ended up in such a strange place. Then the thought occurred to me that one of the children must have put it there during one of their games. I decided to take it home, clean it up and then ask around the village if anyone was missing a cooking pot from their pantry. Just then, Tony appeared from out of the woods brandishing a stick as if it was a pirate's cutlass and then he pretended to run me through with it. Pirates was always his favourite game."

The old man fell silent for a moment or two and looked as if he was close to tears. Michael was beginning to wonder if something bad had happened to Tony.

"Sorry, young man, I wandered off a little didn't I, if I do it again just give me a nudge. Right then, where was I? Oh yes, me and Tony had returned home for tea, playing pirates all the way, of course. Once we had eaten the wonderful meal that my wife had prepared for us – she was the best cook I ever knew – they disappeared into the front room to watch TV whilst I decided to stay in the kitchen and see if I could restore my precious find to its former glory. So I placed it in the sink and filled it with water."

Michael could guess what was coming next.

"As soon as it was full I got my scrubbing brush and plunged it into the pot, ready to give its inside a good scrub, but then, suddenly, the strangest thing happened, the water in the pot began to swirl, faster and faster it went until it began to form a whirlpool. I was quite surprised I can tell you. I looked underneath to see if there was a hole in the bottom that was letting the water out like a plughole, but there was nothing; the bottom of the pot was perfectly intact. When I glanced back inside the pot I got the fright of my life, the water had stopped spinning and was now bubbling away furiously, eventually turning bright green. After a while the surface of the water calmed down and, much to my horror, little orange letters appeared upon it. They moved around randomly before they settled to form a sentence, which read…"

Michael and Harry both spoke at the same time.

"To my new owner, congratulations, you have found the magic cauldron."

Harry looked at Michael pityingly and nodded.

"Of course, you've been through all of this too, then you'll know lad just how terrifying and exciting it is when you first discover the powers of the magic cauldron. At first I couldn't believe what my eyes were seeing. I thought it must have been some kind of joke or an elaborate hoax, particularly as the next sentence that was revealed informed me that I was to receive four wishes, one on each of the next four days. I wrestled with my conscience for a good while I can tell you but eventually something inside of me persuaded me to give it a try. After peeping through the kitchen door into the living room to check that Julie and Tony were still watching TV, I sneaked back into the kitchen and stood in front of the cauldron, poised ready to make a wish. I felt foolish, I was a grown man, an intelligent man, and here I was considering making a wish to a copper pot. The truth was that I didn't for one minute believe that it was going to work, so I just took a deep breath and wished for the first thing that came into my head. I wished that all of the pots and pans from teatime were washed dried and put away. I waited in anticipation as the seconds passed by but nothing happened. I laughed at my foolishness and thanked my lucky stars that no one could see what I was up to. I turned my back and was about to walk away, when all of a sudden a ferocious hissing came from behind me. I spun around and saw that the water in the cauldron had turned scarlet and this time little white letters appeared, they read, "your wish is granted", and then, just like that, the liquid in the pot returned to normal, no one would ever think that it was anything other than a pot full of water. I remember that my heart was beating painfully in my chest and that I'd never been so frightened in all my life but part of me still refused to believe that this could be true. I kept telling myself that this had to be some very clever kind of toy. That was until the magic cauldron began to lift itself slowly out of the kitchen sink. It floated up and across the room, before gently landing itself on the table. The next minute all hell broke loose as, simultaneously, the taps burst into life, filling the sink with water and the washing up liquid bottle tipped itself on its side and squirted a jet of washing up liquid into the sink. I was so terrified that normally I would have fainted but I didn't get the time, I was too busy ducking and diving as plates, cups, knives and forks all whizzed across the room toward the sink, where the dish cloth danced merrily as it cleaned the dishes. After each item had been cleaned spick and span, it would float up into the air and be set upon by the tea towel, before shooting across the room and putting itself neatly away in its respective cupboard. I'm afraid to tell you that I squealed like a little girl and curled up into a ball on the floor for fear of a speeding plate striking the back of my head, but fortunately nothing did. Every item just stowed itself away without bumping into or breaking anything. The tea towel finished the performance by winding itself up and giving my bottom a friendly flick to announce that all was done and then it hung itself neatly on the towel rail. Quickly, I picked up the cauldron and ran upstairs with it. I hid it at the bottom of my wardrobe and covered it with some of my old jumpers. I was determined that no one else would have it, it was my discovery, mine and what's more it still owed me three lovely wishes. I'm sorry to say that despite the fact that the cauldron terrified me, its powers and the promise of wishes coming true was more than I could resist. I'd been corrupted and was overcome by greed."

"It seems to have that effect on adults, you should see my mum and dad, Mum's talking about new shoes and personal trainers, although I don't know why, she's already got several pairs of trainers that she wears for the gym, and, as for Dad, he's even worse. He's already gone on a shopping spree and he's threatening to 'max out his credit cards' whatever that means."

"Good gracious, I didn't realise that your parents were aware of the existence of the magic cauldron, this is more serious than I thought young man. If either of them gets their hands on it next it could have disastrous consequences for us all."

Michael was shocked and gave Harry a very incredulous look.

"Why would it spell disaster? My parents aren't bad people, you know."

"Oh no, that's not what I'm saying," said Harry, quickly backtracking.

"All that I meant was, that in the hands of a child, whose wishes are usually innocent, the damage that the cauldron does isn't too great but, in the hands of adults, and by that I mean any adult, whose wishes tend to be driven by greed, the lust for power or even revenge, the effects of the cauldron can be terribly serious, believe me. I, of all people, should know this, for if I hadn't been so incredibly stupid, I would still have my beautiful wife and young son and I wouldn't be a thirty-four year old, trapped in the body of a much older man."

Chapter Seven

A History Lesson

On hearing this latest revelation, Michael had nearly fallen off of his chair in surprise. He couldn't believe that the man sat in front of him was only thirty-four years old, Michael's own father was thirty-four and he didn't look even half of Harry's age. In fact, with his fluffy white beard, wrinkles and bald patch, Harry looked more like Santa Claus than a young man.

"What happened, Harry, surely you didn't wish to be older, did you?"

"No," chuckled Harry, his little pop belly jiggling as he did so.

"If only I had, then maybe I would still have my beloved wife and son. I'm afraid that it was my third wish that was to be my undoing."

"Your third wish! But you haven't told me what happened with your second wish," said Michael, a little perplexed.

"Haven't I? Deary me, I'm getting really forgetful these days, old age you know. As I was saying, I'd hidden the cauldron in my room, determined to keep it all to myself, then

I returned downstairs to watch TV with my family but I found that I couldn't concentrate. I was incredibly excited and couldn't wait for the next day to come, as I'd already decided what to do with my next wish. I didn't sleep a wink that night, I can tell you. The next morning I performed my best dying swan act and told my wife that I was too ill to go to work and then I rang my employer and told him the same. Once Julie had left the house with Tony, I dashed upstairs and retrieved the cauldron and made my second wish. I wished that I had got more money. Unfortunately, I had failed to specify how much more money I would like, so as I'm sure you would agree, I was less than amused at having taken the day off of work and dashed all the way across town only to find that my bank account had increased by one measly pound."

Michael giggled at this.

"You have to be really careful what you say to it, if you're not specific you end up with a nasty surprise."

"You can say that again," said Harry, nodding in agreement.

"I stormed back home in a terrible mood, I was fuming and it took me several hours to calm myself down and clear my thoughts. Once I was in a better frame of mind, I decided upon my third wish and after having gone through the wording of the wish several times, I was sure that this time everything would be ok."

"What did you wish for?" said Michael trying to hide the excitement in his voice.

"I wished to return to the highest room in the castle that overlooks our village, in the year 1405 AD."

"B…b…b…but why would you do that?" stammered Michael, his jaw hanging wide open.

"Because I'm an historian and at that time I was also the history teacher at the school which you and my daughter attend. History fascinates me, always has, always will and none more so than local history. My particular field of expertise was the history of medicine, so you can imagine my delight when – having spent years researching my family history as far back as I could go – I found that my ancient ancestor was none other than Enryn White, the famous healer and court physician to the king. Now, I know that probably doesn't mean a lot to you, young man but I can assure you that Enryn was a local legend. At a time when healers or doctors would cover you from head to foot in leeches to cleanse your blood or chop off your head to cure your headache, Enryn was dispensing genuine potions that cured people of their ailments. He was also known for his kindness and generosity and, despite the fact that most of his time was taken up looking after the king and his family, Enryn would still find the time to go to the village tavern and help any of the villagers with their illnesses. If he wasn't doing that, he'd be entertaining the local children with wild stories of dragons, witches and knights in shining armour."

"Wow, he sounds really nice."

"He was, and that was partly the reason that I wished to go back and see the great man, but aside from that, there was something that I really wanted to try and retrieve from the past. I wanted to collect a sample of the king's cure."

"What's the king's cure?"

"It was a potion that Enryn had created for the king. He'd tried, without success, for many years to cure the poor king of his terrible headaches. He'd been plagued by them ever since he'd taken a bonk on the head during some battle he'd been fighting in. They were said to be so painful that the king would clasp his head in his hands and scream like a child. The queen was so worried for the king's sanity that she told Enryn that if he was to find a cure he could have anything he wanted in payment. Of course, when he finally did find a cure, Enryn being the Good Samaritan that he was, refused point blank to accept payment."

"But why did you want to bring a sample back with you?"

"Because I foolishly believed that if I could retrieve Enryn's cure for the king and bring it back to the present day, I could make my fame and fortune selling it as a cure for migraines."

Michael was shocked to hear this; he couldn't believe that such a kind man could be capable of doing something so devious.

"Harry, I can't believe that you would think of doing something like that, why it's sort of stealing."

"I know lad and I'm not proud of it," said Harry, hanging his head in shame.

"I wasn't thinking straight at the time, I'd been seduced by greed and had pound signs jumping in my eyes. What's even more unforgivable is the fact that I was fully aware of the dangers of going back in time. If I was to materialise into a tower room full of people, I would probably be arrested and burned at the stake for practising witchcraft or even worse, if I was to do anything that altered history, even in the slightest way, its effects on the future could be devastating.

"But you still went ahead and did it anyway?" said Michael in disbelief.

"Yes, I'm afraid so and it's cost me dearly."

There was a few minutes' pause whilst Harry's mind drifted to thoughts of his loss, and it was only when Michael gave an impatient little cough, that the old man's focus returned to his story.

"I made my wish and this time everything started off the way I'd wanted it to. One moment I was standing in my study, the early morning sunlight pouring in through the window, the next I found myself in a tiny cramped space, in near darkness, surrounded by glass bottles and phials. The only light that entered this space was through a small fleur-de-lys patterned grille. I quickly deduced that I was standing inside Enryn's medicine cabinet, and sure enough, when I peered through the grille, there stood my hero. He was poring through some of his notes and leafing through a huge leather-bound journal. I was as excited as a child at Christmas and couldn't help myself from gasping at the sight before me. Enryn's head suddenly snapped sideways and he stared straight at the cupboard where I was hiding. Terrified, I immediately stepped back, away from the grille and hoped with all my heart that he hadn't seen me. I heard his footsteps approach the cupboard and I braced myself, fully expecting the doors to be flung open, revealing my hiding place, but instead Enryn entered the adjoining cupboard and retrieved something. I gingerly crept back to the grille and saw that the item Enryn had taken from the cupboard was a large copper cauldron. Now I'm here to tell you, young Meeky, that what happened next made the hairs on of my head stand on end."

"What happened, what happened?" exclaimed Michael, bouncing up and down on his chair barely able to contain his excitement.

"Enryn raised his arms up in front of himself, his palms facing forwards toward the cauldron; he stooped his head forward and then began chanting in a language that I'd never heard before. I couldn't believe what was going on in front of me; it appeared as if the old fool was trying to perform magic. Then, all of a sudden, two columns of piercing white light burst forth from Enryn's palms and surrounded the cauldron. It was at least ten minute before he stopped chanting the spell and, as he uttered the last words, the white light unfurled itself, like a snake from around the pot and then disappeared back into the old man's hands. Enryn looked a little unsteady on his feet afterwards, and it was clear that the spell that he had just performed had taken a great deal out of him. Once he'd regained his strength and composure he proceeded to fill the cauldron with water and then he made a wish. Can you guess what he wished for?"

Michael thought about it for a moment or two and then gave up.

"Erm, I don't know, did he wish to be rich?"

"No silly, remember Enryn was a good man. His first wish was to have a potion that would cure his poor master of his terrible headaches. Within minutes, a little round bottle appeared on his table, containing an icy blue liquid. On the bottle was a label, with the words 'the king's cure' written upon it. Just then there was a knock on Enryn's door, and a kind-looking old woman dressed as a lady's maid entered the room. I knew instantly that this must be Enryn's wife Izzabella, who was maid to the queen. Enryn beckoned his wife over and excitedly told her all about his new creation, the magic cauldron, and how he believed that he'd found a cure for the king. She seemed as overjoyed as he was and gave her husband a hug and a kiss on the cheek. She then informed him that the young prince wished to see him. They left the room together and I found myself alone in the tower room with what I'd come for. I opened the cupboard door and tiptoed across the room to the table, where many potion bottles of all colours stood waiting to be dispensed to their particular patient. Each bottle had been carefully labelled with the name of its recipient. In the middle of the table was Enryn's journal, its pages lay wide open enticing me to read; I quickly flipped through the pages and was shocked and rather amused to find that not one of Enryn's cures had been created by scientific means, they had all been the product of his magic."

"Why didn't he tell anyone that he was a wizard, it must have been so cool to be able to do magic," said Michael.

"Ooh, no, no, no, I'm afraid it would have been very uncool to be caught doing magic in those days, in fact the penalty for being caught practising witchcraft was death by burning. So as you can see, he would have had no option but to pretend to be a physician."

"Yes I suppose so, but why did he have to create the cauldron to cure the king when all of his other potions – that had been created by magic from his own hands – had been so successful?"

"I don't know why he couldn't cure the king himself, and nor did he, according to his notes, but it was clear that after many years of trying, he knew he was going to have to come up with something else, hence the cauldron. The truth was that he wasn't very happy about having to produce such a dangerous item. He feared being corrupted by the power of being able to have anything that he wanted, so he limited the amount of wishes that the cauldron could grant to four. He was also adamant that nobody else should get their hands on it. He would keep it hidden away under lock and key and he wouldn't tell a living soul, other than his wife, of its existence. I had to smile to myself and wondered what had gone wrong with his plan seeing as the cauldron had turned up in the whistling tree all those centuries later. Anyway, I finished reading his journal and returned it to the page I had found it on. I then turned my attention to the brightly coloured potions that covered the table top. There was 'Martha's cure for boils' which was ruby red, 'Percy's sneezing tonic' bright green and 'Ezmerelda's flatulence medicine' which was muddy brown."

"What's flatulence?" enquired Michael, puzzled.

"Ehem, er ask your mum," said Harry turning pink.

"There was even a bottle labelled, 'Enryn's daily tonic for rheumatism'. But none of these really interested me; it was the king's cure that I required a sample of. I searched around the table and found an empty glass test tube with a stopper that would be just the job, and then reached over to pick up the phial containing the icy blue cure. Unfortunately, in my haste I knocked over the bottle containing Enryn's rheumatism tonic. My heart nearly stopped as the bottle rolled over the end of the table and crashed to the floor, smashing into a thousand pieces. The fluid bubbled and fizzed angrily and then evaporated away to nothing. I was utterly petrified that someone might have heard the crash and that they would come up here and find the mess that I'd made and then search the castle for the intruder. I started to panic; I found Enryn's broom and quickly swept the broken glass under the table and hoped that no one would notice. Then I found an empty bottle about the same size and shape as the one I'd broken and set about filling it. Enryn's tonic had been deep purple in colour and it took me quite a while, taking small portions out of many of the other potions, before my tonic was about the same colour as Enryn's. I completed it just in time as I heard footsteps coming up the staircase. I ran back to the cupboard and quickly shut the doors behind me. Peeping through the grille, I saw the old wizard enter the room. He was puffing and blowing from the climb up to the tower room and cursing as he rubbed his rheumatic knee. I held my breath as he made a direct line across the room to where the potion that I'd just made lay. He uncorked the bottle and raised it to his lips and then flinched at the smell of it. Puzzled, he lifted the bottle to eye level and gave the fluid a curious gaze. I nearly fainted, as I thought that I was about to be discovered but then the old man just gave a shrug and downed the bottle in one. When at first nothing happened, I gave a sigh of relief and began to relax a little. Then suddenly the wizard began to cough and his face turned an alarming shade of purple. He clasped his head in his hands and shrieked in agony. His eyes rolled back into his head and he collapsed on the floor. He twitched and convulsed in the grip of a violent fit. I watched on in horror, frozen to the spot, unable to move. So much for not altering the past in any way, it was beginning to look like I'd killed my ancestor and if that was the case, then I would soon cease to exist. I could watch no longer, I curled up in the bottom of the cupboard, shut my eyes and hoped that the whole mess that I found myself in would turn out to be a dream and that I'd wake in my own bed, safe and sound. After several hours, Enryn's screams turned into muffled moans and then eventually I heard him pick himself up off the floor and cross the room. I stood up and looked through the grille to see that he'd climbed into bed and pulled the covers up over his head. As the night wore on, the old wizard seemed to settle down and once again I started to let myself believe that things were going to turn out ok after all. It wasn't long until midnight and I couldn't wait to make my final wish and return home. I hadn't managed to obtain my sample of the king's cure but I no longer cared, all I wanted to do was to return to my family and forget the cauldron ever existed. Eventually the hands on my watch ticked past midnight and it was time to go home, but before I went I just wanted to check on Enryn one last time, to make sure that he was ok. I pressed my face to the grille and saw that the long lump under the bedsheets was still there, snoring gently to itself. I was just about to turn away and make my wish, when the wizard pushed down the bedsheets and turned to face me. I gasped in shock as I saw that Enryn was no longer a kind-faced, white-haired, eighty-something year old wizard, but a young man, probably in his twenties, with jet black hair and beard. The instant that he heard me, his eyelids flicked open to reveal two glowing red eyes that shone as brightly as the brake lights on a car. He stared straight at me and I knew for sure that he'd seen me. He leapt from the bed as quick and agile as an athlete. He then gave me a look that will live with me for the rest of my days. His face had evil and malice written all over it and, when he grimaced, he bore a mouth full of pointy white teeth. He then came at me but he didn't walk or run as you or I might, oh no, he floated, his robes billowing around him. I screamed in terror and I only just managed to utter the words 'I wish that I was in my own house at the present day' before he flung open the cupboard door and made a grab for me. There was a bang and then complete darkness. I awoke with a thump and an 'Oooff' as I landed on my sofa in the living room of my cottage. I looked around the room and all appeared to be just as I'd left it. I couldn't believe how stupid I'd been; I'd returned to the past and unwittingly made a potion that had tuned my great ancestor into an evil wizard. I'd completely changed the course of history and yet I'd returned to the present day and everything seemed to be as normal, or so I'd thought, until I noticed these."

Harry held up two very knobbly, wrinkled hands for Michael to see.

"I got up and made to dash for the mirror but my joints were so sore and stiff that I could barely move faster than a snail's pace. When I finally reached the mirror, my worst fears were confirmed. The reflection that I saw was not that of my thirty-four year old self, but that of the ancient man you see sat in front of you now. My heart sank and panic set in when I suddenly realised that the house was empty and my family was nowhere to be seen. I hobbled downstairs, my mind a blur of a thousand possible scenarios. Would my wife be old and grey like me, or worse still, would she still be alive, and my son, where was he, could he have grown up and left home. I looked through the kitchen window on to the back garden to see if I could spot either of them but they were not there. There was however, a football in the back garden, which gave me hope that my son was somewhere around here. I then hobbled back into the living room, to see if I could see any further signs of life, and that's when I noticed it, the huge poster that had taken my whole life to research and fill in. My family tree, framed and in pride of place above the fireplace, where it had always been but this one was different. With my heart in my mouth, I staggered over to the mantelpiece to take a closer look. A sense of despair was beginning to overcome me as I knew deep down what I was going to find when I was close enough to read the poster. My entire family tree had changed. Just like the other tree, the name at the very top was Enryn but that's where the similarities ended, as beneath him I found that I didn't recognise a single name until I reached the last name at the very bottom, which was my name. I was still called Harry Millward but this Harry was seventy-four and had never married or had children. Apparently I was a retired history teacher and an historian and I had an adopted daughter called Toni. As I'd feared, going back in time and meddling with the past had changed the course of history and as a consequence my original family had never existed. I fell to my knees and wept for the rest of the afternoon until I heard the front gate bang shut and saw a little girl walking up the path. She was very upset with me for not meeting her on the bus. I told her that I was very sorry but I was not feeling at all well and I'd fallen asleep all afternoon. The little girl was so concerned for my health and gave me the biggest hug and kiss, which made me instantly love her, and I have come to love her every bit as much as the son that I once had, but there's not a day that goes by that I don't mourn the loss of my wife and child."

Harry's eyes had filled with tears once more and Michael too, felt close to tears, having heard such a terrible story.

"I'm so sorry; I wish that I could do something to help you, Harry."

"As a matter of fact, you can help me Michael, if what I believe is true, we can both help each other."

"Yes, anything, just tell me what to do and I'll do it," said Michael, earnestly.

"You're a good boy, Michael; I'd hoped you might say that. Ok, what I need from you is a promise that you will be determined and brave, because these are the qualities that you will need most if you are to fulfil your destiny as King

Edmund's youngest living male relative, by destroying the cauldron and defeating the evil wizard, the great Enryn Black."

Chapter Eight

The Seven Curses of Enryn

Michael just sat there blinking at Harry, he didn't know what to do or say next. He was beginning to think that the old man was making fun of him. Harry could see that Michael was struggling to comprehend what he'd just been told, so he decided to speak first.

"There's much more to this story lad, like the fact that Enryn Black became so powerful that he overthrew the king and took over his throne. It is written that he ruled the kingdom with terrible violence and fear, I'm afraid my great ancestor was a really naughty man."

Harry considered Michael for a moment, he was going to have to ask some very big favours of him but before he did, there was something that he really must know.

"Before I go any further with the story, I must first ask you a question, is that ok?"

Wearily, Michael agreed.

"Above all else, at this moment in time, what does your heart most desire?"

Michael didn't have to think about his answer twice.

"More than anything, I just want things to go back to how they were before I found that flippin' cauldron, then Mum wouldn't have the press on her back, making fun of her in their papers and Dad would be at work instead of spending a fortune and getting up to goodness-knows-what mischief in town."

"Perfect, an unselfish desire, you thought of other people before yourself, a very rare thing indeed, in fact one might say proof if ever it were needed of your noble blood."

"But what makes you think that I'm related to King Edmund?"

"Well, aside from you remarkable resemblance to him, there's a lot of written evidence in local history books and libraries about the king and his descendants and, being a nosey historian, I decided to study his family tree. I was shocked to find out that he had a relative still living in our village, and that person was none other than my next door neighbour and your uncle."

"Uncle Ed never told us that our great-great-great-great granddad, or whatever, was a king."

"No he wouldn't, I'm afraid that your Uncle Edmund never believed me, but the fact remains that he is a descendant of the king. One day, about a month ago, your uncle came around to see me and said that he'd won the lottery and was moving to Monte Carlo. My first thoughts were that this sounded like a set of circumstances that could probably be linked to a certain mischievous cauldron. He then told me that his brother and his young family would be moving in next door. Excitedly, I asked him if his brother had got a young son and when he said yes, I knew the time had come for the white witch's prophecy to come true."

This was getting more and more bizarre by the minute and Michael found himself struggling to keep up with the story.

"What witch and what prophecy?" squeaked Michael in frustration.

"I'm sorry, do forgive me, I'm getting a little bit in front of myself aren't I. The white witch was none other than Enryn's wife Izzabella. She was a very gifted witch with a special talent for seeing and predicting the future. Very little is written about her before that fateful night when Enryn was transformed; but I do believe that they met as children and learnt the vast arts of magic together throughout their entire lives. This meant that both she and her husband were formidable conjurers, therefore the evil Enryn knew the first person he must get rid of – so that he could continue with his evil plans – was his wife. She didn't go without a fight I can tell you. First of all she transformed herself into a young witch, as she knew that there was no way that she could take on Enryn with her elderly frame. Next, she set about making a weapon that would destroy the cauldron. She feared deeply what would happen if the dark wizard got hold of it. In no time at all she had forged a magic sword that was capable of cutting through the magic cauldron's enchantments and destroying it. Unfortunately Enryn caught her in the act and an epic duel ensued. Sadly, Enryn defeated her and banished her and the sword to the deserted kingdom of ice. One night, many years later, a messenger came to the wizard's court. The mysterious hooded figure had skin that was as translucent as glass and a chill wind followed him wherever he went. He was an ice demon, sent by the white witch with a ball of ice containing a prophecy. The ice demon didn't speak; he just bowed his head and held out the ball of ice for the wizard to take. Enryn snatched the ball and tapped it with his wand, breaking it in two. As soon as he'd done this the witch's voice was released from inside the ice. She told Enryn that she had foreseen the destiny that would befall him should he not change his evil ways and give the kingdom back to its rightful owners. She foretold that one day a brave young boy, who had descended from King Edmund, would destroy the cauldron, undo the seven evil curses that he'd put upon the king's family and their followers, and that he would return to the past and destroy Enryn in combat. The dark wizard was unmoved, he didn't care if the cauldron would be destroyed, he'd already used up all of his wishes acquiring riches and power. As for a boy coming from the future, he believed it not possible and even if it were, what harm could he do to the most powerful wizard of all time. So he continued with his wickedness and the seven curses remain to this day."

"What are the seven curses and how am I supposed to undo them? I don't know the first thing about magic, in fact until a few days ago I didn't think it really existed," said Michael.

"I'm afraid I cannot tell you how to undo them, I do not know, and besides, that is to be your quest; but I can tell you what the seven curses are. The first is the spell he put upon the king and queen. After banishing them from the castle and its grounds, he then cast a terrible curse which turned the king into a troll that must remain underground by day, as trolls turn into stone in daylight, before returning to his human form by night. The queen meanwhile got to spend the day as a human but was transformed into a fox by night. She still roams the woods and gardens at night and I'd wager that if you sat looking through your bedroom window this evening, eventually you would see her. She is the reason that our road is called Foxwood Lane and every house on the lane has been given a name dedicated to the beautiful fox. Enryn cursed the poor king and queen to remain this way forever, this meant that they would still be together but would never see each other as humans for the rest of time. The second curse befell their daughter, Princess Chloe. She was sent to the bottom of the lake to live in darkness for all eternity. The only thing that could save her is if someone agrees to change places with her and whoever would do such a thing as that. Curse number three was put upon the young prince, he was turned into a stone statue, which to this very day, still stands in the middle of the village green. Fourth was a truly wicked hex, which he reserved for the king's army. If you look out of the window, up to the castle, you will see that around its perimeter a neat row of mighty oak trees stand on guard. I'm afraid that's what has become of the king's army. They were turned into trees and given the task of guarding the castle's outer perimeter from intruders, a job I may add, that they do rather well. Next was a spell that was cast upon the villagers that rebelled against Enryn. He turned them into animals of all descriptions. Just imagine, one day you were the big burly village blacksmith, the next you were a slimy toad, unable to do anything but sit on a lily pad and go 'RIBBIT'. The penultimate curse befell the landlord of the village tavern. Enryn knew that the remaining village folk tended to gather there and he suspected that it was a hotbed of rumour and unrest. He feared that the place would become a breeding ground for further rebellion, so he turned the landlord into a werewolf that would prey on the poor unfortunate drinkers that happened to be in there on a full moon. The village tavern eventually turned into the Red Lion pub that you see today and, of course, the original landlord no longer lives there, but be warned lad, the werewolf still returns to this day and will take himself a victim if anyone is fool enough to be caught in the pub or on its grounds when the moon is at its fattest."

"Blimey," said Michael, "I'm not sure I want to know what the last one is, these curses are really scary."

"I know and the last curse is the most powerful and terrifying of all."

Michael just gulped and his knees began to knock.

"Nobody really knows for certain what the last curse is, as it was placed upon the castle and anyone who has entered there from that day on, never came out again. Some say that there's a spirit there that takes people away to another world, others say that the whole castle comes to life, the drawbridge, pictures and suits of armour spring into action and ensnare any poor unsuspecting intruders."

Harry gave Michael a sympathetic smile. The poor lad had come seeking his help and all he'd done was to burden him with more woes. After a short period of silence, Michael spoke up.

"I'll do anything you want Harry, just tell me what to do to get rid of that bloomin' cauldron before Mum and Dad get us all into a load of trouble."

"Good boy, and will you help me break the curses too? There's people around here that's waited more than half a millennium for you to come and free them."

Michael thought about it for a moment. The story of Enryn and the curses terrified him but a part of him knew that it would be the adventure of a lifetime destroying them.

"Yes I'll do it, just tell me what to do first."

Harry clapped his hands together and bounced up and down in his seat, like an excited schoolboy, then suddenly he stopped and the expression on his face told Michael that what he was about to hear was very serious.

"I'm afraid that there is only one way to destroy the magic cauldron and that is with a blow from a sword called Galdrin."

"Is that the sword the white witch made?" enquired Michael.

"That's correct"

"But I thought you said that it was in the kingdom of ice, along with the white witch."

"Correct again, I'm afraid that there is only one way that we're going to be able to acquire that sword, and that is by using your last wish to summon it."

"B…b…but that means that I'll be stuck this way forever, I won't be able to play football or eat pizza and I'll have to wear Boo Boo's silly clothes for the rest of my life," said Michael, beginning to cry.

"I know it's a lot to be asked such a thing and I'm not going to try to force you into doing it either, it has to be your decision, but you have to trust me when I say that things will work out alright in the end."

Eventually, Michael stopped crying. He looked at Harry, who would not return his gaze; he just sat patiently, with his hands folded on his lap, waiting for Michael's decision. He didn't want to spend the rest of his life being mini Meeky, but he was scared of what might happen if one of his parents made a careless wish. If for example, one of them wished that they could return to their youth, then there was every chance that they would do something to change their past and perhaps this would mean that his mum and dad would never meet and, as a result of this, neither he nor Kizzy would ever have been born. There were also other people depending on him and, if what Harry said was true, they'd been waiting a heck of a long time.

"Ok, at the stroke of midnight tonight, I'll make the sword my last wish, but you'd better tell me exactly what to wish for. I don't want to end up spending the rest of my life the size of a salt pot for nothing more than a wooden sword, or something silly."

"No, of course not; that would never do, would it?" said Harry, chuckling.

"It's quite simple, all you have to do is say, 'I wish for the sword Galdrin to come to me' and I'm certain that it will do, for the sword will only appear to someone who is worthy, someone who is selfless and brave, and thinks of other people's needs rather than his own, someone like you Michael."

Harry's praise lightened Michael's mood somewhat and when he dug out a special celebratory bar of chocolate for the occasion, Michael began to feel really good about himself and the quest he now found himself upon.

"Is there anything else that you would like to ask me, young Michael?"

"Yes, there are a couple of things, a moment ago you asked me what my heart most desired, why?"

Harry beamed at Michael, pleased at last to be able to give him some good news.

"I asked you that because it is said that the sword will grant the destroyer of the cauldron whatever their heart most desires, in your case, a return to your life before you discovered the cauldron."

"Whooooopeee, that's brill, I'll be able to play with my toys and ride my bike and drink cans of pop, yeh."

Harry chuckled at the young boy; it was nice to see him happy again.

"I thought that might please you; here, go on, have another crumb of chocolate to celebrate."

Michael stuffed the chocolate into his mouth, filling his cheeks like a hamster.

"The other thing I want to ask you about is your front door. I noticed on the way in that the picture in the glass was of an old man and a king, and I was just wondering if that was supposed to be Enryn and King Edmund. Also your house is numbered seven as well as being called Vixen Cottage, which I thought was really odd, seeing as all the other houses on Foxwood Lane had names, not numbers. Is your house number seven because of the seven curses of Enryn?"

Harry gave Michael a wry smile.

"You really are a clever boy and quite observant too, which is just as well, as these are two of the qualities you are going to need in abundance over the coming years. Now Michael, can I ask just one more small favour of you?"

"Yes, go on then, fire away."

"I'd like you to tell Toni the tale that I've just told you, for I truly believe that you will need her help and that she will be your greatest ally and friend."

"Ok, but why don't you tell her, Harry?"

"I'm afraid I cannot, I couldn't bear to see the look upon on her face when she realised how selfish and stupid I have been. Besides, telling the story will help you both pass the rest of the day until midnight, when, young sir, you and my daughter have a date with destiny."

Chapter Nine

A Magic Sword Called Galdrin

At four o'clock, Michael heard the front gate of Harry's garden, clang shut. He was stood on top of a stack of books that was piled high on the desk in Harry's study room. He'd been waiting there for what seemed like an eternity, for Toni to return home from school, and now he could see her and his mum coming up the garden path. By the look of it, Toni was really pleased to have finished school for the day. She skipped up the path, her face a picture of glee and she positively burst through the front door, sending the old tabby cat, which had been sitting in the doorway to the study, scuttling into the kitchen for cover.

"Dad, I'm home."

At first there was no reply, but then a rather out of breath Harry replied from the kitchen.

"Oh, hello Toni. Good day at school?"

"Not bad, where's Meeky?"

"He's in the study, he's been bursting to see you; I think he's got something he'd like to ask you."

Toni trotted into the study and gazed around in search of Michael.

"Where are you, Michael?"

"I'm over here, on top of your dad's desk." He giggled to himself as Toni's head snapped this way and that, in search of him.

"Whereabouts on Dad's desk?"

"On top of the books, blimey, I think you could do with some specs."

"Ah, there you are, how's your DAY OFF been, hmm?" said Toni, not bothering to hide the tone of sarcasm in her voice.

"It's been great thanks, I've had a cup of tea and I've had some chocolate and pop and your dad told me a really good story."

"Oh yeah, which one's that then?" said Toni beginning to get jealous.

"Never mind that now, I'll tell you later, first there's something I'd like to ask you."

"Ok, go on then," said Toni, eyeing him suspiciously.

"If I can clear it with Mum, would you like to come around and have tea with us and if it's ok with everyone, would you like to have a sleepover as well, I've got some very important stuff that I want to tell you and it needs to be out of earshot of the grown-ups."

"Wow, would I ever, I'd love to come, I've never been to a friend's for tea before, let alone a stopover, wow that sounds so cool, I'll just go and ask Dad if it's ok."

Toni spun on her heels and made for the door.

"Hey, don't forget me."

"Oops, sorry," said Toni, returning to the table and snatching up Michael from his perch on top of the books.

"Hey, steady on, there's no need to squeeze that hard, I know that you're excited but simmer down a bit please."

When they reached the kitchen, they found Michael's mum and Harry chatting over a cup of tea. They'd already discussed the arrangements for Toni to have tea and stop over and Michael's mum had said that it was ok.

As they were leaving Harry's house, Michael noticed that the milkman had been and had left rather a lot of milk.

"Chuff me, you and your dad must like your milk, there's about eight pints there."

"It's not me, it's Dad, he gets through loads of the stuff, he says it's good for his bones but I think he just likes the taste, in fact, I don't know which one drinks more, him or that stray tabby."

"You mean that's not your cat?"

"No, it just appears from time to time, I wish he would shoo it off though, it gives me the creeps, it always seems to appear when I'm on my own and then it just sits there watching me."

Michael found it a bit strange that the tabby wasn't their cat, seeing as they had got a cat flap in the front door. Perhaps Harry just really liked cats, he thought. Michael and Toni spent a really enjoyable afternoon together. First of all they settled in front of the TV and watched cartoons and DVDs. Then, for tea, as a special treat, they ate pizza and fries with loads of red sauce and cola to drink. Next, came pudding which was jelly and ice cream with chocolate chips on top. Mum was in a really good mood and she didn't even get cross when Dad was late getting back from his trip into town. Apparently he'd caught a taxi back home because he'd had, in his words, "a couple of shandies", but judging by the daft expression he was wearing, Michael suspected that he'd had more than just a couple. He was dressed in a very expensive-looking suit, with a dazzling new watch to go with it. Next, he produced from his jacket pocket, a beautiful necklace, which he gave to Michael's mum. He'd obviously gone out and blown an absolute fortune. While his parents were occupied with the necklace, Toni asked Michael for the umpteenth time, what it was that he wanted to tell her.

"I can't say yet, they might hear, I'll tell you at bed time."

Toni was going to be sleeping in his bed, whilst he himself had been furnished with a clean sock for his sleeping bag, which was placed under his desk. This was done for his own safety as it sheltered him from the prospect of being squished by Toni, should she need to get up and go to the toilet in the night.

Michael's mum tucked the two children into their respective beds and wished them sweet dreams. She was just about to flick the light switch as she left the room, when Toni asked if she could have the light left on and the door left open.

"I get really scared if I'm shut in and it's dark."

Mum agreed, she switched on Michael's night light, left the door open and even left the landing light on, before disappearing into her own room to join her husband, who was now snoring like a bull moose. Michael was about to start teasing Toni about her fear of the dark but, when he saw how embarrassed she looked, he chose to be sympathetic instead.

"I don't really like the dark either but I'm getting used to it, I just keep telling myself that Mum and Dad are just down the corridor and they won't let anything bad happen to me."

"I'm not really scared you know, it's just that I can't sleep when the lights are off, that's all," said Toni, trying to defend her pride.

"Anyway, never mind all that now, are you going to tell me this secret or not?"

"Yes but come over here and fetch me, I'm having to shout at the top of my voice so that you can hear me and I'm starting to go hoarse."

Toni got up and fetched him and then returned to sitting on his bed, with Michael sat cross-legged on her palm. He began to recall the whole of the day's events, of how he went to see Harry, in the hope that he might help him, but instead he was told an incredible story of wizardry and witchcraft of cauldrons and curses. Toni just sat in silence and listened carefully to every word that Michael said. He was beginning to worry as he knew that there were parts to this story that might deeply upset Toni, but nevertheless he knew he had to carry on. When Michael had finished telling the story, he timidly bowed his head and gazed at his feet, waiting for a reaction from Toni. She said nothing and, when he looked at her, she wore a completely blank expression on her face but he could tell that something was welling up inside of her, ready to explode. Then suddenly it did.

“WOOOOPPEEEEEE!” she roared. “That’s so cool. Wow, what an adventure we’re going to have on this quest, I can’t wait.”

And with that, she flung her hands up into the air in triumph. Unfortunately she’d forgotten that Michael had been sat in the palm of her hand. He found himself catapulted skywards at a horrific rate of knots, and his ascent was only halted when his bottom made heavy contact with the ceiling. Then came the downwards journey.

“Waaaaaaa!” screamed Michael as he plummeted back to earth almost as quickly as he’d gone up.

Thankfully, Toni had realised her mistake and quickly held out Michael’s pillow for him to land on.

“You, you, you BLOOMIN’ TRUMP, what the heck did you do that for, you nearly gave me a heart attack,” gasped Michael, his eyes still bulging with terror.

“Sorry, I got a bit excited, I didn’t think what I was doing, anyway stop moaning, I caught you didn’t I which means that I saved your life, so you owe me big time Meeky.”

“Bah,” said Michael sulkily. He folded his arms, turned his back on her and that’s when he saw Kizzy. She was in the middle of the floor, staring at them, her twinkling eyes ablaze with excitement.

“Oh blimey, how long has she been there?”

“Dunno, I didn’t hear her come in,” said Toni, looking a little shaken. Just then, Kizzy squealed and clapped her hands.

“Me like that storwey.”

“Oh bum, we’d better shut her up, she’s going to wake the whole house.”

Michael thought that he knew Kizzy all too well and fully expected her not to budge an inch until she’d been read another story, but what she did next completely stunned him.

“Kizzy look after Mummy and Daddy, Meeky Moo go smash up nasty cauldron.” And with that, she toddled off to her room. The two children looked at one another, gobsmacked.

“Well, that’s me well and truly freaked out,” said Toni, still staring at the doorhole that Kizzy had just disappeared through.

"Agreed, the sooner we get rid of that thing the better," said Michael.

Eventually, the moment that they'd been waiting for arrived. The bright red numbers on Michael's clock flicked to midnight and it was time to make his wish. Toni placed him on top of his desk and took a couple of steps back out of harm's way. Michael approached the giant cauldron and once more it came to life, jiggling and vibrating in anticipation as it felt him draw near. Michael took a deep breath and spoke slowly and clearly.

"I wish for the sword Galdrin to come to me."

From where he stood, Michael could hear the contents of the pot bubbling and hissing but he wasn't tall enough to see what was going off inside.

"Lift me up Toni, please."

Toni gingerly approached the desk. She'd had the cauldron spit at her before now and she was keen not to be subjected to a repeat performance. She picked him up and held him at arm's length. He could see that the cauldron was going through its usual procedure but this time the sentence that appeared in the fizzing liquid read, "Your final wish is granted." Then instead of the scarlet liquid returning to the colour of ordinary water, it exploded out of the cauldron and into the air, forming a red mist that slowly evaporated into the atmosphere.

"Woa!" screamed the two children simultaneously.

Then, with bated breath, they awaited the appearance of the sword. They waited and they waited, hearts beating fast, not knowing what to expect, but nothing happened. Michael didn't understand and he was beginning to panic. Had he just used up his last wish for nothing, he certainly hoped not as he was depending on the sword to return things to the way they were.

He was on the verge of giving up when suddenly his bedroom window flung itself open and an icy blast of wind entered the room, carrying with it a woman's voice, which said, "The cauldron has granted you your wish, the sword Galdrin is now in your world, you must go and collect it as the cauldron will not willingly summon its destroyer. That which you seek can be found in a tree that whistles. Go, go quickly before someone else finds it and all is lost."

As soon as she had stopped speaking, the wind died down and his window gently closed itself. Toni and Michael just gave one another a knowing glance.

"Do you suppose that was the white witch's voice?"

"Yes, I guess so, and by the sound of it, she wants us to go and get the sword, like right now," said Michael.

"I'm not sure I like the sound of that, it's really dark and creepy in those woods at night and the whistling tree is right in the middle."

"I know, I can't say I'm looking forward to the journey either but you heard what she said. I suppose if we're on a quest, it's bound to get scary sometimes."

Toni agreed and the two of them got dressed and crept downstairs as quickly as they could. Toni put on her jacket and placed Michael in her top pocket. She was worried that she might stumble and have to put out her hands to save herself and if Michael was in one of them, she would either drop him or squash him. Besides, he was still wearing Boo Boo's T-shirt and shorts, so he'd be warmer in her pocket. Michael pointed to where Dad hung his keys. They were on a hook by the back door. Toni unlocked the door and slipped out into the night air. It was the height of summer, so it wasn't too cold outside but it was quite a cloudy night which made it very dark. Fortunately, Toni knew her way around very well, she'd explored every inch of these woods and would probably have found her way with her eyes shut. She was very quiet and Michael could sense that she was every bit as frightened as he was. She crossed the rickety rope bridge and entered the dark woods. Toni was right; the woods were a very creepy place to be at night. He couldn't believe how noisy the place was at this hour. Leaves rustled, branches creaked and groaned, and small creatures darted about in the thick undergrowth. On more than one occasion, he could have sworn that he saw beady eyes peering down at him from up in the trees. As they went deeper and deeper into the woods, the trees became more densely packed. Occasionally, Toni would have to push the branches aside to stop them hitting her in the face. She climbed a steep slope to where a huge rock was perched precariously between two others. Michael guessed that this must have been the rocking stone and was about to ask Toni to tell him about it, when suddenly a flock of bats shot out from the dark space beneath the rock and frightened the life out of the pair of them. Toni ran as fast as she could, ducking under branches, and jumping over tree roots and small streams. Eventually they came to a clearing, in the middle of which stood a huge oak tree. It looked very old and Michael could clearly see the face of an old woman in its trunk, with its two dark eyes and its mouth, puckered up ready to whistle. Toni approached the tree very slowly and then stopped, rooted to the spot, like a rabbit in the headlights.

"What's wrong?" said Michael.

"I don't like this; I get the feeling that we're being watched."

"Well we probably are, there are a thousand and one creatures in these woods and I'm sure that some of them are bound to be watching us, they're probably as scared as we are, can we just get on with this and find the sword please; I want to get out of here as quickly as we can."

"Agreed," said Toni.

She approached the tree and gingerly stuck her head in the first eye socket. After peering around for a few seconds, she declared that there was nothing in there and so moved on to the next eye. She was just about to insert her head into the trunk a second time, when a pair of glowing amber eyes appeared out of the darkness, just inches in front of her nose. Toni shrieked and took a couple of steps back. Michael looked on in horror as the eyes lazily surveyed them and then moments later a little owl, no bigger than a teacup, waddled out of the darkness and stood perched on the edge of the eye socket.

"Phew, it's only a stupid owl," said Michael feeling relieved, that was until the owl spoke.

"Ayup mate, who do you think you're calling stupid?"

This time both children screamed.

"Well that's bloomin' nice isn't it, how would you like it if I screamed when I saw your face."

And with that, the little owl gave them both a very snooty look and took off into the woods.

"I blame you for all of this you know," said Toni, prodding her top pocket where Michael was stood quivering. "I've lived around here for years and before you turned up I'd never clapped eyes on a magic cauldron or a flippin' talking owl."

"Oh shut up and stick your head in that next hole will you, it's bound to be in there," said Michael testily.

Toni chose not to argue and just got on with it. She drew a deep breath and shoved her head into the mouth hole.

"Brrr, it's freezing cold in here."

"Never mind that, can you see the sword?"

Toni continued to look around but saw nothing.

"I can't see it anywhere, perhaps it's in the second one, I didn't get the chance to look properly, oh, no, hold on a minute, there is something in here."

Toni withdrew her head from the tree and examined the item she'd just found.

"Bah, it's nothing more than a darning needle." She was just about to toss it away when Michael squeaked at her to stop.

"Look more closely, that's no needle, it's a sword."

Toni eyed it more closely.

"Ooh yes, but how are you going to destroy the cauldron with this? It's tiny."

"I don't know but the prophecy says I do, so that's good enough for me, 'ere can I have a look at it please?"

Toni passed him the sword. To her, the weapon was merely pin-sized, but to Michael it was just right. He brandished it and swung it around like a knight at a medieval tournament.

"Very impressive, Sir Meeky Moo of the round tiddlywink-sized table."

"Oi, stop taking the micky," said Michael, giving her a prod with the sword.

"Ouch!" squeaked Toni. She was about to get her revenge by giving his head a little squeeze between her thumb and forefinger, when the woods around her suddenly brightened up. The two of them looked up to the sky and saw that the wind was sweeping away the clouds to reveal the moon; A FULL MOON. Just then, from somewhere not very far away, came a blood-curdling howl; a howl that could only belong to a werewolf.

Chapter Ten

Kizzy and the Cauldron

Michael and Toni had never been so terrified. Toni spun on her heels and fled for their lives, she didn't know that she was capable of running this fast but fear was driving her forward. Branches whipped her face, cutting her as she fled, but she felt nothing, she just continued to charge. She flew down the hill, past the rocking stone and leapt a small brook, but it was no good, she could hear the werewolf gaining on her and when it gave a piercing "Aaaawooooo" she could tell that it was only a few feet behind her. She turned her head and glanced over her shoulder and saw a dog that was as big as a bear. Its lips were pealed back, its teeth bared and its eyes were as red as coals in a fire.

"Toni, watch out." Michael cried out but it was too late, Toni looked forwards just in time to see a huge tree root sticking up from the ground in front of her.

She kicked it and fell head over heels. She flipped herself on to her back so as not to crush Michael in her breast pocket and saw the wolf pounce, its claws out ready for the kill. Just then, something big leapt from the bushes just to her left and head butted the werewolf in its side. It tumbled sideways and rolled down a steep bank, yelping and howling as it went. Michael peered out of Toni's coat pocket and saw that the creature that had just rescued them was a huge stag. It was the most beautiful animal that he had ever seen. Its soulful eyes fixed them with a steady stare, and then it spoke.

"Go now, quickly, and don't stop until you reach the safety of your house. I fear that old Arthur down there has only been stunned and he will be angrier than ever when he returns."

"Oh, ok thank you," stammered Toni as she clambered to her feet and began to run once more.

"Are you ok?" shouted Michael.

He was worried that she had hurt herself in the fall as she was now limping. She didn't reply as her lungs were burning and she was gasping for breath. From behind them, they could hear a commotion going on and Michael knew that it must be the stag trying to hold off the werewolf. Toni hobbled across the rope bridge and into the orchard at the bottom of Michael's garden.

"Aaaawoooo!" Came the cry from behind them and they knew for sure that the werewolf was once again pursuing them.

By now Toni was crying and she was wincing with pain with every step that she took. Her pace was slowing dramatically and by the time that they were halfway up the lawn, the werewolf had exited the orchard and was tearing up the garden path after them.

"Come on Toni, you can do it, you're so brave, just a few more steps to go now."

Michael couldn't remember whether or not they had locked the back door when they left the house earlier but he hoped with all of his heart that they hadn't, if they had to fumble with the lock to get in, they were done for. Toni limped up the steps, grabbed the door handle and flung open the door. In her haste to get inside, she tripped over the doorstep and once again she was forced to flip herself on to her back to protect Michael. She looked through the open doorway and was confronted by the sight of the werewolf leaping toward her. She kicked the door shut with her good leg and watched as the huge creature slammed into the door's glass window. It stood up and shook its head, in a daze, and then gave a mighty roar as it beat its chest in fury. Then it turned on its heels and bounded off into the night. Toni curled up into a ball on the floor and began to cry her eyes out. Michael felt so sorry for her; this was all his fault and he wished that he could think of something to say or do to comfort her but he didn't know how. The only thing that he could think of was destroying the cauldron and then hopefully things would turn out to be ok.

"I can't believe how brave you've been tonight Toni, you're the bravest person I've ever met, you're really tough too, there's no way I could have done what you've done tonight."

"Thanks," sniffed Toni.

"I promise that everything will be alright, I just need you to take me upstairs to the cauldron and then I'll destroy it and everything will return to how it was before I found the horrid thing."

Toni said nothing for a moment or two before slowly getting to her feet, wincing and yelping as she did so.

"Come on then, let's get this over with," said Toni through gritted teeth. It took her an age to climb the stairs as every step caused her injured knee great pain but she didn't give up. Eventually they reached Michael's room.

"Shut the door behind us please, Toni, I don't know how loud it's going to get when we destroy the cauldron but it's sure to wake Mum and Dad up; in fact I'm amazed that we haven't woken them already."

Toni gently closed the door and then placed Michael on top of his desk, beside the cauldron.

"Well, here goes then," said Toni, passing Michael the sword.

He reached up and took the sword from her but as soon as his hand closed around the hilt of the sword, an icy white light exploded in front of his eyes, followed by a series of images that showed him the history of the sword, from its creation by Izzabella, the spell that she had used to turn herself into a beautiful young witch, the duel with Enryn and then the centuries that she and the sword had spent together in exile in the kingdom of ice. It all flashed before Michael's eyes.

"Woa, did you see that?"

"See what?" said Toni, giving him a puzzled look. "All I saw was you grabbing the sword."

"Oh, well it let me see its life story; I think it's trying to tell me that it's time to bring the tale to an end."

Michael drew a deep breath, held the sword aloft and then charged at the cauldron with all of his might. The cauldron wasn't going to go that easily though, as Michael took his swing with the sword the pot simply slid across the desk out of reach. Michael and Toni looked at one another in disbelief.

"It looks like you're going to have to be a bit quicker than that, give it another go."

Michael clenched his teeth and this time he flew at it with even more force than before, but once again the cauldron just slid out of his way. He was beginning to lose his temper and he charged at it again, screaming as he went. This time the cauldron changed its tactics and instead of sliding, it flew at him. Michael had to duck to avoid being knocked off the top of his desk. He spun around just in time to see it making a return attack. This time he wasn't quick enough and the cauldron struck him in the middle of his back, sending him flying through the air. He screamed as he tumbled head over heels, he saw the bedroom floor approaching him fast and he braced himself for the impact that would probably kill him. Just then a hand wrapped around him and stopped him, inches from the ground. Toni had dived across the bedroom and caught him. Once again she had saved his life. They both landed with a thump, the impact sending the sword flying out of his hand. He watched helplessly as it scuttled across the carpet and then slid through the gap at the bottom of the door and out on to the landing.

"Grrr, why can't anything ever be simple?" grumbled Michael.

"Don't worry, I'll go and get it," said Toni. She pushed herself up into a sitting position and was about to get to her feet when the cauldron made another dive bomb attack, striking her on the head with horrific force. The blow made a sickening sound and Toni slumped on to the carpet unconscious. The cauldron then settled itself in the middle of the floor and sat there vibrating, as if to taunt him.

"TONI!" screamed Michael.

He squeezed himself out of her clenched fist and went over to her in the hopes of resuscitating her but he was too small. He could see from where he stood that she'd already got a large lump on her forehead and it was bleeding heavily. It was clear that she needed hospital attention and quickly but what could he do, he was incapable of opening the door and his feeble little screams couldn't be heard more than a few feet away. Michael began to cry, Toni had saved his life on several occasions tonight and now that she badly needed him, he was powerless to help. So much for him being destined to destroy the cauldron, cure the curses and defeat Enryn; he couldn't even help a friend in need. Just then, Michael heard something shuffling on the carpet, the other side of his bedroom door and he froze in terror. After all he'd been through these last few days, he wasn't sure that he could bear anything else sinister happening to him. He strained his cars, trying to make out what was on the other side of the door. Whatever it was, he could hear it getting closer and closer and soon all that separated him from whatever horror that lay beyond, was a couple of inches of wooden door. He was just about to start backing away, when the creature spoke to him.

"Kizzy give icle Meeky his stick back to smash the nasty potty with."

And with that, his baby sister poked the sword back under the door. This time Michael didn't have to be told what to do, he just leapt on the sword, spun around and threw it at the cauldron. It struck the pot right in the middle, its blade sticking in to about three quarters of its length. From this point, two large cracks opened up and a piercing white light shone from within. Next came a huge bang; louder than anything Michael had ever heard before, and then everything went black.

Suddenly Michael felt his toe strike something hard and he fell all of his length, landing with an "OOOFF" amongst the fallen apples. He shook his head; he felt dazed and confused and couldn't understand what had happened to him. Only moments ago, he'd been in his bedroom, at night, trying to destroy the cauldron but now he found himself in an orchard, on a hot sunny day. He massaged his throbbing toe and looked all around him to see what had tripped him and that's when he realised what was going on. He'd travelled back in time to the exact moment that he'd discovered the cauldron, only this time the object that he'd tripped on was nothing more than an old tree root. The cauldron was nowhere to be seen, it had been destroyed. Michael lay back in the grass and heaved a huge sigh of relief. Harry had been right; everything was going to be ok. He smiled to himself when he realised that he'd gone back to Friday afternoon and for everyone else but him, the events of the last four days had never happened. At this point, he hadn't met either Toni or Harry and he chuckled to himself when he pictured all the fun he was going to have reintroducing himself to them and telling them his story so far. Michael picked himself up and ran back into the house. Dad was sat at the table reading his newspaper and Mum was busy trying to get Kizzy to eat her baby food. Michael told his parents about the rope bridge, the tree swing and the castle but nothing more, they would only tick him off for telling lies and, besides, the quest was going to be a secret between himself, Toni and Harry. He was so excited when he thought of all the adventures that were still to come. Getting rid of the cauldron had been dangerous and exciting enough, so just imagine what fun he was going to have undoing the seven curses.

When his dad saw how happy and excited Michael looked, he smiled to himself and said, "So you think that you might get to like it here after all, then?"

"Yes, I think it's really cool here, Dad."

"Good, and oh, I forgot to tell you, there is a little boy lives next door called Tony, he's the same age as you and I think he likes football too."

"Toni's not a boy, she's a girl."

“Oh, right, sorry, I was just assuming that with a name like Toni, she was a boy. Anyway how do you know that she’s a girl, have you already met?”

“Yes we have, sort of,” said Michael, smiling to himself.

“Can I go and call for her?”

“No, you’ve got your unpacking to do first, I’ve already taken your case up for you; it’s in your new room which is just at the top of the stairs and then turn…”

But Michael cut him off mid-sentence.

“Yes, I already know where it is, Dad.”

His dad just gave him a puzzled look, then shrugged his shoulders and went back to reading his paper. Michael thundered up the stairs and looked through his bedroom window he could see a football shooting up into the air. He couldn’t wait until he could go around and call for Toni, but this time, he thought to himself, maybe he wouldn’t challenge her to a game of football.

The End